How the Two Ivans Quarrelled

and Other Russian Comic Stories

Translated by Guy Daniels

ONEWORLD CLASSICS LTD
London House
243-253 Lower Mortlake Road
Richmond
Surrey TW9 2LL
United Kingdom
www.oneworldclassics.com

'The Tale of How Ivan Ivanovich Quarrelled with Ivan Nikiforovich'
first published in Russian in 1834
'A Panegyric in Memory of My Grandfather' first published in Russian
in 1792
'A Tale of How One Muzhik Looked after Two Generals' first published
in Russian in 1869
'The Eagle as Patron of the Arts' first published in Russian in 1884
'The Tale of Ivan the Fool' first published in Russian in 1886
These translations first published, together with other stories, in the US
in the volume *Russian Comic Fiction* by New American Library in 1970,
and later reprinted by Schocken Books in 1986

These revised translations, with a revised introduction, first published
by Oneworld Classics Ltd in 2011

Translation, introduction and notes © Guy Daniels, 1970

Cover image © Getty Images

Printed in Great Britain by CPI Antony Rowe

ISBN: 978-1-84749-173-2

Contents

Introduction   3

A Note on the Translations   13

The Tale of How Ivan Ivanovich   15
Quarrelled with Ivan Nikiforovich (N. Gogol)
    Chapter the First   17
    Chapter the Second   24
    Chapter the Third   37
    Chapter the Fourth   44
    Chapter the Fifth   59
    Chapter the Sixth   66
    Chapter the Seventh   75

A Panegyric in Memory   87
of My Grandfather (I. Krylov)

A Tale of How One Muzhik   103
Looked after Two Generals (M. Saltykov)

The Eagle as Patron of the Arts (M. Saltykov)   117

The Tale of Ivan the Fool (L. Tolstoy)   133

Notes   171

Introduction

The true homeland of comedy is a
despotism without too many gallows.

Stendhal, *Racine and Shakespeare*

F OR OUR AUSLÄNDER'S STEREOTYPE of Russian literature
as unrelievedly gloomy, we can blame other things
besides our own ignorance: above all, the vagaries of
the Russian comic spirit. The brilliance and vigour of
that spirit cannot be called into question. Throughout
the history of pre-revolutionary Russian literature, it
enjoyed undisputed supremacy on the stage. Without
exception, the few eighteenth-century Russian plays that
remain worthy of mention are comedies, from Fonvizin's *The Hobbledehoy* and *The Brigadier General* to
Kapnist's *Chicane* and Krylov's *Trumf*. And so are the
two greatest plays of the nineteenth century: Griboye-
dov's *Woe from Wit* and Gogol's *The Inspector General*. Again, most of the major poets, from Derzhavin
through Krylov, Pushkin and Lermontov, to Nekrasov,
were masters of comic verse, as were numerous minor
poets, like A.K. Tolstoy. But in the realm of Russia's
greatest literary achievement, the novel, the behaviour
of that comic spirit has been decidedly skittish. Except
for a few brief visits to the dark abodes of Dostoevsky's

3

novel-tragedies, it has pretty much avoided the domain of the "Great Prose Realists"; and for all the splendour of that one isolated edifice, *Dead Souls*, the "Russian comic novel" as a genre unto itself can hardly be said to exist.

The same is true of short fiction. There are plenty of humorous sketches (Chekhov alone wrote hundreds of them) but only a few first-rate comic stories. Hence the limited scope of this collection. Indeed, of the authors represented here, only one – Gogol – was primarily a creator of comic fiction. Indeed, in a sense Gogol was *the* creator of the comic short story, and 'How the Two Ivans Quarrelled' (1834) is perhaps the best, and certainly the first, masterpiece of its kind.

It is a sobering thought that one of the gloomiest periods in Russia's history – the reign of the "pewtery-eyed" Nicholas I (1825–55) – produced its greatest comic genius, Nikolai Gogol. And it is not only sobering but dismaying to reflect that Nicholas, who was the sworn enemy of Lermontov and contrived to make the last years of Pushkin's life miserable, sometimes just couldn't seem to do enough for Gogol. He personally intervened, for instance, to permit the first production of *The Inspector General*; and during the writing of *Dead Souls* he responded to Gogol's appeals for financial help with two handsome grants. Now the "Prussian Tsar" was occasionally obtuse; and this trait of his is nowhere more evident than in these magnanimous gestures – considering the ultimately devastating social effect of the two works in question. On the other hand, we can be sure that when the already demented Gogol – some five years before his death by self-imposed starvation – published his infamous *Selected Passages from Correspondence with Friends* (1847), its abject eulogy of autocracy came as no surprise to Nicholas. The book's shock effect was reserved for the author's radical friends – like Belinsky, whose outrage and dismay were vented in his celebrated letter to Gogol.

It was Belinsky who first recognized Gogol's stature as an artist and called public attention to it – in an article centred upon *Mirgorod*, Gogol's second collection of Ukrainian stories, which included 'The Two Ivans'. For this alone he deserves something better than the downgrading of him that has become fashionable among us. I was therefore much gratified, upon looking again at Vladimir Nabokov's marvellous (and often misleading) book on Gogol, to rediscover in it a spirited defence of Belinsky against the "little conceptions" of "some modern American critics". Elated by this unexpected moral support, I turned for further enlightenment to Vladimir Vladimirovich's comments on Gogol's Ukrainian stories.

Those comments led off with an abrupt dismissal of Gogol's first collection, *Evenings on a Farm near Dikanka* (1831–32) whose "charm and fun have singularly faded". True enough. So I settled back in pleasurable anticipation of some deep and delightful insights into *Mirgorod* – and particularly into those two masterful tales that established Gogol's fame as a maker of comic fictions: 'The Two Ivans' and 'Old-World Landowners'.

And what did I learn? I learnt: 1) that Gogol is *not* a humorist; 2) that his misconceived fame as such is based solely on those faded *Evenings* – except that: 3) it is also based on *Mirgorod*; 4) that both *Evenings* and *Mirgorod* leave Nabokov "totally indifferent" – except that: 5) when he reread the former it *didn't* leave him totally indifferent.

Well. If made by a lesser author, such muddle-headed pronouncements would of course be beneath one's notice. But when they occur in an otherwise brilliant book by perhaps the most "prestigious" author of our times, duty demands that we hoist the red flag signalling "Danger!"

Nabokov's *Nikolai Gogol* is in some ways the most important – and by all odds the best-written – book on its subject. That it should be read goes without saying. What doesn't go without saying is that it is also the worst possible introduction to the Gogol of 'The Two Ivans' and 'Old-World Landowners'.

The best introduction is still the one penned by Belinsky, in his article 'On the Russian Short Story and the Short Stories of Mr Gogol', which appeared in *The Telescope* in 1835. Struck by Gogol's tremendous originality, Belinsky came up with a phrase which still serves, perhaps better than any other, to mark the watershed between the literature of the old school and modern fiction – of which Gogol and Sterne are the greatest forerunners. In 'Old-World Landowners', 'The Two Ivans' and 'The Nose', said Belinsky, Gogol "made everything out of nothing".

Exactly. In 'Old-World Landowners', as in a play by Beckett or Ionesco, *nothing happens*. The old couple just "drink and eat, and eat and drink and then, as people have done since time immemorial, die". This is what Belinsky calls "spareness of plot" (*prostota vymysla*). The real matter of the story lies elsewhere: in that marvellous alchemy by which the "nothing" of everyday trivia somehow becomes "everything"; and in Gogol's uneasy, ambivalent vision of the world, with a backdrop of gloom behind every comic bit.

In 'Old-World Landowners' these elements are fused into a perfect work of art, appropriately low-keyed. In 'The Two Ivans' they are jumbled together – in an unbridled exuberance precluding perfection but making for greater comedy – with whatever else comes to hand. One of these odd items is a wild parody of a Flemish painting in which the action has "only one spectator: the boy in the enormous frock coat, who stood rather quietly picking his nose". Another is a bit of authentic Marx Brothers madness: "Ivan Ivanovich is of a rather timid character. Ivan Nikiforovich, on the contrary, wears big, baggy trousers..." And while he's at it, Gogol stands E.T.A. Hoffmann on his head and makes even the fantastic trivial and vulgar (not to say unlovely). He has done this before; but never so well as when Ivan Nikiforovich's petition is spirited away from the courtroom by Ivan Ivanovich's brown sow, who thereby breaks a deadlock and wins fame as literature's first *suinus ex machina*.

How now, brown sow? Are you no more than a fat adjunct to a skinny plot? Far from it! Close inspection reveals that it was the sow who set the whole thing in motion, when she (or the offer of her by Ivan Ivanovich in exchange for a gun) aroused the ire of Ivan Nikiforovich. For Ivan N. (like Gogol) was hypersensitive to hogs, the care and feeding of which, in the rural Russia of those days, was the *exclusive province of women* – towards whom Ivan N. (like Gogol, again) was even more hypersensitive. Not only that, but in textbook terms she "symbolizes the theme" of the whole story: swinishness, or, in contemporary parlance, slobism.

7

Gogol is the world's greatest virtuoso in the depiction of slobism (*poshlost*). The "height of this degradation" (to quote Lermontov) is of course reached in *The Inspector General* and *Dead Souls*, but the phenomenon had fascinated Gogol since early in his career. Witness the old couple in 'Old-World Landowners' and the two Ivans – both of them consummate slobs, yet rivalled by all the minor characters in the story, and even excelled by the incomparable Agafya Fedoseyevna, who "ate boiled beets in the morning, talked scandal and swore wonderfully well".

But if Gogol ranks first, he is still merely *primus inter pares*, since slobism was the favourite theme of Russian satirists generally, and his mentors were many. Chief among them were Fonvizin (one of whose characters preferred pigs to people) and Krylov. In particular, Gogol employs in 'The Two Ivans' the same basic device used by Krylov in his satire of *poshlost*: the "false panegyric", whereby a naive narrator, in the course of praising his hero, "inadvertently" reveals all the latter's slobism.

But this was just one of many techniques employed in a story that was much more complex in its authorial attitudes than Krylov's 'Panegyric'. Gogol was decidedly not a clear-eyed son of the Enlightenment; nor was he an "exposer" like Saltykov or an "anti-exposer" like Dostoevsky in 'The Crocodile'. More than anything else, he was an artist fascinated by the ambivalence of his own view of things, and expressed it in a subtle (not to say sly) interplay between pity and parody. In Belinsky's words:

Indeed, to make us take the liveliest interest in the quarrel between Ivan Ivanovich and Ivan Nikiforovich – to make us laugh to the point of tears at the stupidities, worthlessness and imbecility of these living lampoons of mankind – is amazing. But then to make us pity those idiots – pity them with all our hearts – and take leave of them with a kind of deep melancholy, exclaiming along with him: "It is dreary in this world, gentlemen!" – *that* is the divine art that is called creativity.

There were two brief periods during the reign of Catherine the Great (1762–96) when satirical journalism flourished – when there were not "too many gallows". The earlier period (roughly, 1769–74) began with the founding by Nikolai Novikov of the first of his two satirical magazines. It ended rather abruptly when Novikov became too outspoken on such subjects as serfdom and corruption in high places.

The second period began about 1789, when a young man of twenty named Ivan Krylov, who had already written a number of keen-edged comedies, founded a satirical publication of his own. By all rights that period should have ended almost as soon as it began – in 1790, when Catherine, thrown into a panic by the French Revolution, imprisoned such "troublemakers" as Novikov and Alexander Radishchev – and might well have, but for the courage of the young Krylov. Even though his first publication closed down amid the wave of arrests, the undaunted Krylov promptly founded another, in the pages of which he was too outspoken on almost everything. This second period ended, in effect, in 1792, when the police descended on the printing establishment of "Krylov and Associates" and put the young troublemaker under surveillance. It is characteristic of Krylov that he went on to launch a third journal the following year. But things were getting much too hot, and he had to leave St Petersburg in a hurry. He didn't return to the capital until some thirteen years later, in the reign of Alexander I – about the time he began to write the fables that would bring him world fame.

One of the many astounding things about Krylov is that before he was twenty-five he was writing satirical prose pieces that place him among the most outstanding "sons of the French Enlightenment" in Russian letters. Of course, most of the other significant writers of Catherine's reign were also nourished on the ideas of the French Enlightenment, but in their satire they did not venture beyond the persiflage of courtiers' (or merchants') manners and morals. Krylov, though hardly so radical as Radishchev, did not hesitate to ridicule arrogance and injustice wherever he found them: if on the throne, why then, so much the worse.

But for all his gifts as a writer of prose, Krylov's favourite medium since earliest youth had been poetry; and in about 1806 he returned to a genre he had dabbled in earlier, the verse fable. In no more than a few years he emerged as the greatest fabulist of modern times, and the most popular – at any rate in nineteenth-century Russia, where his *Fables* ranked second only to the Bible in sales.

Mikhail Yevgrafovich Saltykov (1826–89), often referred to as "Saltykov-Shchedrin", his pen name, was born into a family of provincial gentry. Following a period of exile in Siberia for his radical writings, he returned to European Russia and rose in the civil service. In his forties, still an unreformed radical, he retired to devote himself full time to writing and editing *Notes of the Fatherland*.

A particularly partisan spirit marks (and often mars) Saltykov's work, so much so that his fictions often degenerate into mere journalism. Most of them, moreover, were written in "Aesopic" (allusive) language in order to circumvent the censors; and this, too, tends to detract from their survival value as literature. In fact, the only one of his longer works completely free of such blemishes is *The Golovlyov Family*, an impressively gloomy novel of the chronicle type which ranks second only to his fables.

Although a good many of the latter are topical, they often rise (as Krylov's verse fables always do) to a level of universal application, and so endure. In 'The Eagle as Patron of the Arts', for instance, the Eagle is plainly identifiable as the Tsar (at first Alexander II, then Alexander III), and the Falcon as the liberal minister, Loris-Melikov; yet this fable still holds up as an attack on autocracy in general – and, for that matter, on such pseudo-concepts as "the Great Society". But 'How One Muzhik Looked after Two Generals' is something rather different. Saltykov's chief target here is an entire social class: the high-ranking civil servants. And his secondary target is another, since his muzhik, far from being the idealized peasant who abounded in the more dreary "social protest" literature of the times, is clearly an "Uncle Tom", however sympathetically portrayed. Saltykov, in short, was a good deal more realistic than the kind of radical writer who specialized in grim documentaries while taking the "natural goodness" of the peasants for granted.

Tolstoy himself lapsed into this kind of naivety on occasion. There is certainly a good dollop of it in 'Ivan the Fool', for instance. (Or perhaps there only appears to be. In this marvellous realm of make-believe, you simply can't tell. Nor does it matter.)

Tolstoy's 'Ivan the Fool' belongs to the same period as Saltykov's 'Eagle', the middle Eighties, a period of repression, stagnation and "little deeds", as one Russian writer put it – and autocracy is certainly one of its chief targets, along with the State in general, militarism, unenlightened self-interest and (naturally) culture. But Tolstoy, like Chekhov, had never been one to engage in journalistic feuds, and his attitude towards the "enemy" is the farthest thing from either wrath or spitefulness. It is, rather, one of Olympian contempt – as witness his female soldiers defeating a vast army of males by heaving bombs out of as yet uninvented aeroplanes.

Needless to say, this kind of outlook is incompatible with the *lachrymæ rerum* from which Gogol's comic art is distilled in the *Mirgorod* stories. (Not that Tolstoy lacked compassion: but he chose to express it in works of a different kind – for example, in 'The Death of Ivan Ilych', published the same year as 'Ivan the Fool'.) Still, it does serve to lift his comic-anarchist tract to a high place in that "literature of satirical exposure" that put up sprouts in the reign of Catherine the Great, then withered until briefly revived in the middle and late decades of the nineteenth century, only to die in the era of Stalin, when there were "too many gallows".

A Note on the Translations

Of all "classical" Russian prose, Gogol's is notoriously the most difficult to translate. To be sure, some of the other original texts used in preparing this volume presented special problems of their own, but those obstacles are as nothing when compared to those set up for the translator by Gogol: confusing switches in tense, Ukrainianisms, and even grammatical errors. ("You try to correct it, and you spoil it", wrote the lexicographer Vladimir Dahl to the historian Mikhail Pogodin. "What would happen if he wrote Russian?")

Besides all the foregoing difficulties (too abundant to be enumerated here), 'The Two Ivans' contains not a little legal gibberish, most of it archaic. In particular, the third petition – the one penned by the "scribbler" who "had three quill pens stuck behind each ear" – is nine parts nonsense: nothing is harder to translate than that. I have done my best, though, to keep this nonsense intact – along with the awkward switches in tense elsewhere in the story.

At the same time, I have tried to respect – as some translators have not – that eloquence for which Ivan Ivanovich was famous in Mirgorod. It is nothing less than a slander upon that worthy citizen to have him say in his petition things like "lawfully criminal actions" (Garnett) or "legally criminal acts" (Magarshack). Ivan Ivanovich may

13

well have been a slob, but he was a *literate* one. And what he did say was that the other Ivan's acts were *zakono-prestupnyye*, which *looks* like "lawfully criminal" etc., but is actually an archaic form of "illegal"; i.e. a "stepping over" (*prestupleniye*) of the law (*zakon*).

The "sly Ukrainian", as Pushkin called Gogol, is a very tricky writer. I only hope he hasn't tricked me too often.

The Tale of How Ivan Ivanovich Quarrelled with Ivan Nikiforovich

Nikolai Gogol

Chapter the First

Ivan Ivanovich and Ivan Nikiforovich

WHAT A FINE FITTED COAT Ivan Ivanovich has! Really splendid! And what astrakhan! Hell and damnation, what astrakhan! Dove-grey, with a touch of frost! I'll bet nobody else has that kind! For the love of Heaven, just look at it! Especially when he stops to talk to somebody. Just look at it from the side. How delicious! Indescribable! Velvet! Silver! Fire! Great God! Nikolai the Wonder-Worker, Holy Saint! Why don't I have such a coat? He had it tailored before Agafya Fedoseyevna went to Kiev. You know Agafya Fedoseyevna – the one who bit off the assessor's ear?

Ivan Ivanovich is an excellent man. What a house he has in Mirgorod! A slanting porch roof supported by tall oak posts runs all the way around it, and everywhere under this roof are benches. When it gets too hot, Ivan Ivanovich takes off both his coat and his underclothes, leaving on nothing but his shirt, relaxes on his porch, and watches what is going on in the yard and out in the street. What apple and pear trees he has under his very windows! Just open the window, and the branches push their way into the room. All this is in front of the house; but you should see what he has in the garden! What *doesn't* he have?

Plums, red cherries, sweet cherries, all kinds of vegetables, sunflowers, cucumbers, melons, sugar peas – even a granary and a forge.

Ivan Ivanovich is an excellent man. He is very fond of melons. They are his favourite food. As soon as he has dined and come out on the porch in nothing but his shirt, he tells Gapka to bring him two melons. He slices them himself, collects the seeds in a special piece of paper, and begins to eat. Then he orders Gapka to bring him the inkpot, and in his own hand he writes an inscription on the paper containing the seeds: "This melon was eaten on such-and-such a date". If a guest was present, he adds: "So-and-so participated".

The late judge of Mirgorod always admired Ivan Ivanovich's house when he looked at it. Yes, it's quite a nice little house. What I like is that sheds and outhouses have been added all around it, so that if you look at it from a distance you can see only roofs piled on top of one another, very much resembling a plateful of pancakes – or, better still, the kind of fungi that grow on trees. The roofs, moreover, are all thatched with reeds; and a willow, an oak and two apple trees lean on them with their spreading branches. Little windows with carved, whitewashed shutters can be glimpsed through the trees, and even reach out as far as the street.

Ivan Ivanovich is an excellent man. Even the commissioner from Poltava knows him. When Dorosh Tarasovich Pukhivochka comes from Khorol, he always goes to see him. And the archpriest, Father Pyotr, who lives in Koliberda, whenever he has a few people at his home, always says he doesn't know anyone who fulfils his Christian duty and knows how to live like Ivan Ivanovich does.

18

Lord, how time flies! Even then, more than ten years had gone by since he had become a widower. He didn't have any children. Gapka has children, and they often run about in the yard. Ivan Ivanovich always gives each of them a *bublik*,* or a slice of melon, or a pear. His Gapka carries the keys to the storerooms and the cellars. But Ivan Ivanovich himself keeps the key to the big trunk that stands in his bedroom, and the one to the middle storeroom; and he doesn't like to let anyone in there. Gapka, a healthy wench, goes about in a kind of slit skirt of woollen homespun. She has fine, robust calves and fresh cheeks.

And what a devout man is Ivan Ivanovich! Every Sunday he puts on his fitted coat and goes to church. When he has entered and bowed in all directions, he usually takes a place in the choir loft and joins in the singing with a good bass. When the service is over, Ivan Ivanovich absolutely cannot bear to bypass the beggars. Perhaps he would have preferred not to bother himself with this tiresome business, were he not impelled to do it by his natural goodness.

"Good day, poor woman," he would say, when he had sought out the most crippled old woman in a tattered dress all made up of patches. "Where do you come from, poor creature?"

"From the farm, my lord. It's going on three days now since I've had a bite to eat or a drop to drink. My own children turned me out."

"Poor thing! But why did you come here?"

"Why, to beg, sir. To see if somebody might give me enough for a crust of bread."

"Hm! Well then, I suppose you want bread?" Ivan Ivanovich would ask.

19

"Oh, yes! I do! I'm hungry as a dog!"

"Hm!" Ivan Ivanovich would answer. "And perhaps you would like some meat too?"

"Why, I'll be glad for anything you're kind enough to give me."

"Hm! Would you be thinking that meat is better than bread?"

"It's not for a hungry person to choose. Whatever you kindly give will be good." So saying, the old woman would hold out her hand.

"Well, get along now – go with God," Ivan Ivanovich would say. "Why are you still standing there? I'm not beating you, am I?" And having addressed similar questions to one or two more, he finally goes home – or else drops in on his neighbour, Ivan Nikiforovich, or the judge, or the mayor,* to have a glass of vodka.

Ivan Ivanovich likes it very much when someone gives him a present or gift of some kind. This pleases him very much.

Ivan Nikiforovich is also a very fine fellow. His yard is next to Ivan Ivanovich's yard. They are such close friends as the world never produced. Anton Prokofyevich Pupopuz, who to this day goes around in his brown frock coat with the light-blue sleeves and dines at the judge's on Sunday, used to say that the Devil himself had tied Ivan Ivanovich and Ivan Nikiforovich together with a rope. Where one went, the other would drag himself along too. Ivan Nikiforovich was never married. It used to be blabbed about that he had got married, but this was an absolute lie. I know Ivan Nikiforovich very well, and I can affirm that he never had any intention of getting married. Where do all these slanders come from?

For instance, there was a rumour that Ivan Nikiforovich had been born with a tail in the rear. But this invention is so absurd – and at the same time so disgusting and indecent – that I don't even think it necessary to disprove it to enlightened readers, who undoubtedly know that tails in the rear are found only on witches (and on very few of them, at that) – who, moreover, belong rather to the female sex than to the male.

In spite of their great mutual affection, these two rare friends were not altogether alike. Their characters can best be gathered from a comparison. Ivan Ivanovich has the unusual gift of speaking in an extraordinarily pleasant manner. Lord, how he can talk! The sensation can only be compared with that produced when somebody is feeling your head for lice, or gently scratching your heel. You listen and listen until your head droops. Pleasant, surpassingly pleasant! Like a nap after taking a bath. Ivan Nikiforovich, on the contrary, mostly says nothing. But if he does drop a remark, just look out! It will cut better than any razor. Ivan Ivanovich is tall and skinny; Ivan Nikiforovich is somewhat shorter, but well spread out in breadth. Ivan Ivanovich's head is like a radish with the tail down; Ivan Nikiforovich's head is like a radish with the tail up. It is only after dinner that Ivan Ivanovich lolls on the porch in nothing but his shirt: in the evening he puts on his fitted coat and goes somewhere – either to the town store, which he supplies with flour, or to the countryside to catch quail. Ivan Nikiforovich lies on his porch all day (if it isn't too hot a day, he usually lies with his back to the sun) and never goes anywhere. If he happens to think of it, in the morning he will walk through the yard and look things over; then he'll go back to rest.

21

In the old days he used to drop in on Ivan Ivanovich. Ivan Ivanovich is a man of most unusual refinement: in polite conversation he never utters an improper word, and he is quick to take umbrage if he hears one. Ivan Nikiforovich sometimes isn't too careful with his language. When this happens, Ivan Ivanovich usually stands up and says, "Enough, enough, Ivan Nikiforovich! Better go on out into the sun than to utter such ungodly words!" Ivan Ivanovich gets very angry if there's a fly in his borscht: he goes into a rage, shoves the soup plate away from him, and gives his host a tongue-lashing. Ivan Nikiforovich is extremely fond of bathing, and when he is sitting in water up to the neck, he orders the tea table and samovar to be set in the water too; and he is very fond of drinking tea in such coolness. Ivan Ivanovich shaves his beard twice a week; Ivan Nikiforovich shaves his once. Ivan Ivanovich is extraordinarily inquisitive. God forbid you should start to tell him a story and not finish it! And if he is displeased with something, he lets you know right away. From Ivan Nikiforovich's countenance it is hard to tell whether he's pleased or angry; even if he is overjoyed at something, he won't show it. Ivan Ivanovich is of a rather timid character. Ivan Nikiforovich, on the contrary, wears big, baggy trousers with such broad folds that if they were inflated you could put the whole yard into them, along with the granaries and outhouses. Ivan Ivanovich has big, expressive eyes the colour of tobacco, and a mouth that looks something like the letter V. Ivan Nikiforovich has little, yellowish eyes, completely concealed by his thick brows and chubby cheeks, and a nose that resembles a ripe plum. When Ivan Ivanovich offers you a pinch of snuff, he always licks the lid of his snuffbox first, then taps it with his finger and, having proffered it, says, if you are an acquaintance, "May I make so bold, sir, as to ask you to do me the favour?" Or if you are not an acquaintance: "May I make so bold, sir – not having the honour of knowing your rank, your name, or your patronymic – to ask you to do me the favour?" Ivan Nikiforovich, on the other hand, puts his snuff horn right in your hands, and merely adds: "Do me the favour." Both Ivan Ivanovich and Ivan Nikiforovich detest fleas. Therefore, neither Ivan Ivanovich nor Ivan Nikiforovich ever lets a Jewish pedlar pass by without purchasing from him various little jars of a remedy against those insects – having first abused him roundly for professing the Jewish faith.

Despite certain dissimilarities, however, both Ivan Ivanovich and Ivan Nikiforovich are excellent men.

Chapter the Second

*From Which One May Learn What Ivan Ivanovich
Coveted, the Subject of a Conversation between Ivan
Ivanovich and Ivan Nikiforovich, and How It Ended*

O NE MORNING – in July, it was – Ivan Ivanovich was
lying on his porch. The day was hot, the air was dry
and shimmered. Ivan Ivanovich had already been out in
the countryside to see the mowers and his farm, and had
already questioned the muzhiks and peasant women he
met as to where they were coming from, where they were
going, and why. He was terribly tired, and had lain down
to rest. Lying there, he looked around at the storehouses,
the yard, the sheds, the hens running about in the yard,
and thought, "Good Lord! What a clever proprietor I
am! Is there anything I don't have? Fowl, outbuildings,
granaries, something to satisfy every whim; fruit and berry
brandies; pears and plums in my orchard; poppies, cab-
bages and peas in my garden... Is there anything I don't
have? I'd like to know if there's anything I don't have!"

Having asked himself that profound question, Ivan
Ivanovich became lost in thought. Meanwhile, his eyes
were seeking out new objects: they passed over the fence
into Ivan Nikiforovich's yard, and were involuntarily attracted by a curious spectacle. A gaunt peasant woman
was bringing out, one after another, garments that had
been stored away and hanging them on a clothes line to

air. Soon an old uniform with frayed facings had stretched out its sleeves in the air, and was embracing a woman's brocade jacket. Sticking out from behind them was a gentleman's uniform with crested buttons and a moth-eaten collar, then a pair of stained white cashmere trousers that had once been pulled on over Ivan Nikiforovich's legs, and now could scarcely be pulled on over his fingers. Next, another pair of trousers were quickly hung up in the shape of an inverted V. Then came a dark-blue Cossack-style jacket that Ivan Nikiforovich had had made for himself twenty years before, when he was getting ready to join the militia and had already grown a moustache. Finally, to top it all off, a sword was displayed, looking like a spire sticking up in the air. Then the fluttering skirts of something resembling a grass-green kaftan with copper buttons the size of a five-copeck coin. From behind the skirts peered a vest trimmed in gold braid and cut low in front. The vest was soon blocked from view by the old-style petticoat of a deceased grandmother, with pockets big enough to hold a watermelon apiece. All this mixed together constituted a very interesting spectacle for Ivan Ivanovich, while the sun's rays, picking up here and there a dark-blue or green sleeve, the red trimming on a cuff, or a bit of gold brocade, or playing on the sword-spire, made it into something extraordinary, like the puppet shows* put on in the villages by strolling actors. Especially when the crowd of peasants, pressing close together, watches Herod in his golden crown, or Anton leading his goat: behind the scenes a fiddle scrapes, a Gypsy slaps his hands against his lips in lieu of a drum, as the sun goes down and the fresh coolness of the southern night imperceptibly snuggles up to the fresh shoulders and breasts of the plump village girls.

Soon the old woman came out of a storeroom, grunting and dragging along an ancient saddle with broken stirrups, worn-out leather holsters, and a saddlecloth that had once been scarlet, with gold embroidery and copper discs.

"That's a stupid woman!" thought Ivan Ivanovich. "Next thing, she'll drag out Ivan Nikiforovich and air him out."

As a matter of fact, Ivan Ivanovich was not entirely wrong in his guess. Some five minutes later, Ivan Nikiforovich's baggy nankeen trousers were hung up, filling almost half of the yard. After that, she brought out a cap and a shotgun.

"What does that mean?" Ivan Ivanovich wondered. "I've never seen a shotgun at Ivan Nikiforovich's. What is he up to? He never hunts, but he keeps a shotgun! What does he need it for? But it's a fine little thing. I've been wanting to get one like that for a long time. I'd very much like to have that little gun. I like to amuse myself with a nice little gun."

"Hey there, granny!" Ivan Ivanovich shouted, wiggling his forefinger.

The old woman came up to the fence.

"What's that you have there, old girl?"

"You can see for yourself – a gun."

"What kind of gun?"

"Who knows what kind? If it was mine. I s'pose I'd know what it's made of. But it's the master's."

Ivan Ivanovich stood up and began to examine the shotgun from every angle – and forgot to reprimand the old woman for hanging it and the sword out to air.

"It's made of iron, I'd say," the old woman went on.

26

"Hm! Iron. Why should it be iron?" Ivan Ivanovich said to himself. "Has your master had it for a long time?"

"Could be for a long time."

"A fine little thing!" Ivan Ivanovich continued. "I'll ask him for it. What does he need it for? Or I'll trade him something for it. Tell me, granny, is your master at home?"

"Yes, he is."

"What's he doing? Lying down?"

"He is."

"Very well. I'll come and see him."

Ivan Ivanovich got dressed, took his gnarled stick to keep off the dogs (since in Mirgorod there are many more dogs in the street than people), and went.

Although Ivan Nikiforovich's yard was next to Ivan Ivanovich's, and you could climb over the fence from one into the other, Ivan Ivanovich went by way of the street. From the street you had to go through an alley so narrow that if two one-horse carts happened to meet in it, they couldn't make way for each other but had to remain in that position until someone took hold of the back wheels of each and dragged it back into the street. As for anyone on foot, he would be adorned both by the burdocks and the flowers growing along the fence on either side. At one end of the alley stood Ivan Ivanovich's cart shed; at the other stood Ivan Nikiforovich's granary, gate and dovecote.

Ivan Ivanovich went up to the gate and rattled the latch. Within, dogs began barking; but when the motley-coated pack had seen the familiar face, they ran back with their tails wagging. Ivan Ivanovich walked across the yard, made colourful by the Indian pigeons fed from Ivan

Nikiforovich's own hand, the melon and watermelon rinds, a patch of grass here and there, a broken wheel in this place or that, or a barrel hoop, or a lolling little boy in a dirty shirt – a picture of the kind that painters love! The shade from the clothes hung out on the line covered almost the entire yard, and gave it a degree of coolness. The old woman met him with a bow, gaped, and just stood there. The front of the house was ornamented by a little porch whose roof was supported by two oak posts – an unreliable protection against the sun, which at that time of year in Little Russia* shines in earnest and bathes anyone out walking in a hot sweat, from head to foot. From this it was plain to see how great was Ivan Ivanovich's desire to obtain that indispensable article, when he decided to go out in that kind of weather, even changing his set custom of strolling out only in the evening.

The room that Ivan Ivanovich entered was quite dark, since the shutters were closed. A sunbeam coming through a hole in one of the shutters took on the hues of the rainbow and, striking the opposite wall, painted on it a varicoloured landscape of thatched roofs, trees and the clothes hung out on the line – the whole thing upside down, however. All this endowed the room with a kind of marvellous twilight.

"God's blessing!" said Ivan Ivanovich.

"Ah, how do you do, Ivan Ivanovich!" answered a voice from a corner of the room. Only then did Ivan Ivanovich see Ivan Nikiforovich lying on a rug spread out on the floor. "Pardon me for being in a state of nature."

Ivan Nikiforovich was lying there with nothing on at all – not even a shirt.

"That's quite all right. Have you slept today, Ivan Nikiforovich?"

"I have. And have you slept, Ivan Ivanovich?"

"I have."

"And so you have just now got up?"

"*Just now got up?* Good Heavens, Ivan Nikiforovich! How could I sleep until now? I've just come back from the farm. The grain fields along the road are splendid. Marvellous! And the hay is so tall, soft and golden!"

"Gorpina!" Ivan Nikiforovich shouted. "Bring Ivan Ivanovich some vodka and fruit pastries with sour cream."

"Fine weather today."

"Don't praise it, Ivan Ivanovich! The Devil take it! There's just no getting away from this heat."

"So you just had to mention the Devil! Ah, Ivan Nikiforovich! You'll remember what I told you, but then it will be too late! You'll pay the price in the next world for your ungodly words!"

"How did I offend you, Ivan Ivanovich? I didn't mention your father – or your mother, either. I can't understand how I offended you."

"Enough, now! Enough, Ivan Nikiforovich!"

"I swear I didn't offend you, Ivan Ivanovich!"

"It's odd that the quail still don't come at the bird call."

"As you like. Think what you want, but I didn't offend you in any way."

"I don't know why they won't come," Ivan Ivanovich said, as though he hadn't heard Ivan Nikiforovich. "Could it be that it isn't quite the season yet? But this *should* be the time."

"You say the grain looks good?"

"Marvellous grain! Marvellous!"

After this there was a silence.

"Why is it you're hanging the clothes out, Ivan Nikiforovich?" Ivan Ivanovich finally asked.

"Well, that damned old woman let mildew get into those splendid clothes – almost new, they are. Now I'm airing them out. The material is fine, really excellent. They just have to be turned, and I can wear them again."

"I saw one thing there I liked very much, Ivan Nikiforovich."

"What was it?"

"Tell me, please. What need do you have for that shotgun that was hung out to air along with the clothes?" At this point Ivan Ivanovich proffered his snuffbox. "May I make so bold as to ask you to do me the favour?"

"No, thanks. Help yourself. I'll take a pinch of my own." So saying, Ivan Nikiforovich felt around and found his snuff horn. "That stupid woman! So she hung the shotgun out there too, did she? Fine snuff that the Jew in Sorochintsy makes. I don't know what he puts in it, but it's so fragrant! A little like balsam. Here, take some. Put it in your mouth and chew it a little. Take some – do me the favour!"

"Tell me, please, Ivan Nikiforovich – I'm still speaking of the shotgun – what are you going to do with it? After all, you don't need it."

"What do you mean I don't need it? I might go hunting."

"Good Heavens, Ivan Nikiforovich! When will you go hunting? At the Second Coming, no doubt. So far as I know and others can recall, you haven't yet killed so much as one duck. Besides, the good Lord didn't fit you out with a constitution for hunting. You have a dignified bearing and figure. And how can you go dragging yourself

30

through the marshes when that garment of yours, which it is not proper to call by its name in polite conversation, is still being aired out? No, you require rest and relaxation." As was mentioned above, Ivan Ivanovich spoke in an unusually picturesque manner when it was necessary to convince somebody of something. How he could talk! Lord, how he could talk! "Yes, dignified behaviour is the thing for you. I say, give it to me!"

"The very idea! That's a valuable shotgun. You can't find guns like that anywhere today. I bought it from a Turk, way back when I was getting ready to go into the militia. And now I'm supposed to give it away all of a sudden? The very idea! It's an indispensable thing!"

"Indispensable for what?"

"What do you mean, 'for what'? Why, if robbers attack my house... Not indispensable, indeed! Now, thank the Lord, my mind is at ease and I'm not afraid of anybody. Why? Because I know I have a shotgun in the storeroom."

"A fine shotgun! Why, Ivan Nikiforovich, the lock on it is ruined!"

"What do you mean? What's ruined? It can be fixed. I just have to put a little hemp oil on it to keep it from rusting."

"From what you are saying, Ivan Nikiforovich, I can see that you have no kindly disposition towards me whatsoever. You don't want to do anything for me as a token of friendship."

"How can you say, Ivan Ivanovich, that I show you no friendship? You should be ashamed! Your cattle graze on my pastureland, and I've never once laid hands on them.* Whenever you go to Poltava, you ask me for the use of my light carriage. Well? Have I ever refused it?

31

Your youngsters climb over the fence into my yard and play with my dogs, and I never say anything about it. Let them play, just as long as they don't touch anything. Let them play!"

"If you don't want to make me a present of it, perhaps we could trade something."

"What will you trade me for it?" And Ivan Nikiforovich propped himself up on his elbow and looked hard at Ivan Ivanovich.

"I'll give you my brown sow – the one I fed up in the sty. A splendid sow! Just see if she doesn't give you a litter of pigs next year."

"Ivan Ivanovich, I don't know how you can say such a thing! What do I need your sow for? To give a funeral banquet for the Devil?"

"There you go again! You just can't get along without the Devil! It's sinful of you! By Heaven, it's a sin, Ivan Nikiforovich!"

"Really, Ivan Ivanovich! How could you, in exchange for my gun, give me the Devil only knows what – a sow!"

"Why is she 'the Devil only knows what', Ivan Nikiforovich?"

"Why? Just judge for yourself. This is a shotgun – a thing everybody knows. But that's the Devil only knows what – a sow! If anybody else but you had said it, I might have taken it as an insult."

"But what have you noticed that's wrong with the sow?"

"Really, now! What do you think I am? To take a sow—"

"Sit down! Sit down! I'll forget it… Keep your shotgun! Let it rot and rust standing in the corner of the storeroom! I don't want to talk about it any more."

After this came a silence.

"They say," Ivan Ivanovich began, "that three kings have declared war against our Tsar."

"Yes, Pyotr Fyodorovich was telling me. What kind of a war is it? And what's it about?"

"Nobody can say for sure, Ivan Nikiforovich, what it's about. My guess is that the kings want all of us to adopt the Turkish religion."

"They're fools! What a thing to want!" declared Ivan Nikiforovich, raising his head.

"So you see, our Tsar has declared war on them because of that. 'No,' he says. '*You* adopt the *Christian* faith!'"

"What do you think, Ivan Ivanovich? Our men will beat them, won't they?"

"Oh, yes. So you won't trade the little gun, Ivan Nikiforovich?"

"You amaze me, Ivan Ivanovich. You're supposed to be well known for your learning, yet you talk like you're still wet behind the ears. That I should be such a fool—"

"Sit down! Sit down! Forget the gun! Let it fall to pieces! I won't talk about it any more!"

At this point the refreshments were brought in.

Ivan Ivanovich drank a small glass of vodka and ate a fruit pastry with sour cream.

"See here, Ivan Nikiforovich. Along with the sow, I'll give you two sacks of oats. After all, you didn't sow any oats. One way or another, you'll have to buy oats this year."

"I swear, Ivan Ivanovich, a person shouldn't talk to you except when he's eaten a bellyful of peas." (That was nothing: Ivan Nikiforovich comes out with expressions much worse than that.) "Who ever heard of trading a shotgun for two sacks of oats? I'll bet you won't toss in your astrakhan coat."

"But you're forgetting, Ivan Nikiforovich, that I'm giving you the sow besides."

"What? Two sacks of oats and a hog for a shotgun?"

"What's wrong? Isn't that enough?"

"For a shotgun?"

"Of course, for a shotgun."

"Two sacks for a gun?"

"Two sacks – not empty, but full of oats. And have you forgotten the sow?"

"Go kiss your sow! Or if you don't want to, go kiss the Devil!"

"Oh, you *are* touchy, aren't you? You'll see! In the next world they'll pierce your tongue with red-hot needles for saying such ungodly things! After talking with you, a person has to wash his face and hands and fumigate himself."

"Excuse me, Ivan Ivanovich, but a gun is a noble thing – the most fascinating kind of amusement. And besides, it's a very pleasing ornament to a room…"

"You, Ivan Nikiforovich, have been fussing over that shotgun of yours *like an idiot child with a new toy*," said Ivan Ivanovich with vexation; because he had really begun to get angry.

"And you, Ivan Ivanovich, are a regular *goose*."

If Ivan Nikiforovich had not uttered that word, they would have quarrelled and then parted friends, as always. But now something very different happened.

Ivan Ivanovich flushed all over. "What was that you said, Ivan Nikiforovich?" he asked, raising his voice.

"I said you were like a goose, Ivan Ivanovich."

34

"How dare you, sir, ignoring both propriety and re-spect for a man's rank and family, insult me with such an abusive name?"

"What's abusive about it? And, for that matter, why are you flapping your hands so much, Ivan Ivanovich?"

"I repeat. How did you dare, flouting all decency, call me a goose?"

"I spit on your head, Ivan Ivanovich! Why have you set up such a cackling?"

Ivan Ivanovich had lost all self-control: his lips were quivering; his mouth lost its usual shape of the letter V and became a kind of O; his eyes blinked so much it was frightful. This happened to Ivan Ivanovich very seldom – only when something had made him really furious.

"Then I hereby inform you," declaimed Ivan Ivanovich, "that I do not want to know you!"

"A great loss that is! By Heaven, I won't weep for that!" Ivan Nikiforovich answered.

He was lying, lying! I swear he was lying! He was very upset by it.

"I will never set foot in your house again!"

"Aha, ha!" said Ivan Nikiforovich, so vexed he didn't know what to do and, against all habit, rising to his feet. "Hey, woman! Boy!"

At this, the same gaunt old woman appeared in the doorway, along with a small boy muffled up in a long, ample frock coat. "Take Ivan Ivanovich by the arm and show him the door."

"*What? To a gentleman?*" Ivan Ivanovich cried out with a feeling of injured dignity and wrath. "Just you dare! Come on! I'll annihilate you and your stupid master to-gether! The crows won't be able to find where you lie!"

(Ivan Ivanovich spoke with unusual force when his soul was shaken.)

The group as a whole presented a striking picture: Ivan Nikiforovich, standing in the centre of the room in his full beauty without any adornment whatsoever! The old woman, gaping, with the most senseless, terrified look on her face. Ivan Ivanovich with his arm upraised, as the Roman tribunes are depicted. It was a rare moment! A magnificent spectacle! And yet there was only one spectator: the boy in the enormous frock coat, who stood rather quietly picking his nose.

Finally, Ivan Ivanovich picked up his cap. "Fine behaviour on your part, Ivan Nikiforovich! Excellent! I won't let you forget it!"

"Get along, Ivan Ivanovich! Get along! And make sure you don't cross my path! If you do, Ivan Ivanovich, I'll beat your mug to a pulp!"

"Just for that, take *this*, Ivan Nikiforovich!" replied Ivan Ivanovich, making a fig at him* and slamming the door – which gave a shrill creak and opened again.

Ivan Nikiforovich appeared in the doorway and tried to add something, but Ivan Ivanovich rushed out of the yard without looking back.

Chapter the Third

*What Happened after the Quarrel between
Ivan Ivanovich and Ivan Nikiforovich*

A ND SO TWO WORTHY MEN, the pride and ornament of
Mirgorod, had quarrelled. And because of what?
Because of a mere nothing – a goose. They refused to see
each other, they broke off all relations – although formerly
they had been known as the most inseparable of friends!
Every day, Ivan Ivanovich and Ivan Nikiforovich used to
send to enquire about each other's health; and they often
talked to each other from their respective porches, and
said such pleasant things to each other that it gladdened
the heart to hear them. On Sundays, Ivan Ivanovich in
his fitted astrakhan coat and Ivan Nikiforovich in his
Cossack-style kaftan of brown nankeen would set out
for church almost arm in arm. And if Ivan Ivanovich,
who had exceedingly sharp eyes, was first to notice a
mud puddle or filth of any kind in the street (which *is*
sometimes found in Mirgorod), he would always say to
Ivan Nikiforovich, "Be careful, and don't step here, because it's not good." For his part, Ivan Nikiforovich also
manifested the most touching signs of friendship, and no
matter how far away he was standing, he would always
hold out his snuff horn towards Ivan Ivanovich, saying,
"Do me the favour." And what well-managed households

and lands both of them had!... And these two friends...
When I heard of it, I was thunderstruck. For a long time I
simply wouldn't believe it. Ivan Ivanovich has quarrelled
with Ivan Nikiforovich! Such worthy men! After that, is
there anything solid left in this world?

After Ivan Ivanovich got home, he remained for a long
time in a highly excited state. Usually, he first went to the
stable to see whether the mare was eating her hay. (Ivan
Ivanovich had a grey mare with a bald patch on her fore-
head – a very fine horse.) Next he would feed the turkeys
and suckling pigs with his own hand. Then he would
go into the house, where he would either make wooden
dishes (he was very skilful, and could fashion various
articles from wood as well as any turner) or read a book
published by Lyuby, Gary and Popov* (Ivan Ivanovich did
not remember the title of the book, because a servant girl
had long since torn off the upper part of the title page
by way of amusing a child), or else rest on the porch. But
now he didn't busy himself with any of his usual pastimes.
Instead, when he encountered Gapka, he began to scold
her for dawdling about doing nothing, though in fact
she was hauling buckwheat into the kitchen; he threw a
stick at a rooster that had come to the porch for his usual
tribute; and when a grimy urchin in a torn shirt ran up to
him and cried, "Daddy, Daddy! Give me a honeycake," he
stamped his foot and threatened him so fiercely that the
frightened little boy ran off God knows where.

Finally, however, he thought better of it, and began to
busy himself with his usual activities. He sat down to
dinner late, and it was almost evening when he lay down
to rest on the porch. The good borscht with pigeon in it
that Gapka had cooked made him completely forget what

had happened that morning. Ivan Ivanovich once again began to survey with pleasure his little domain. At length his eyes came to rest on his neighbour's yard, and he said to himself, "I haven't been to Ivan Nikiforovich's yet today. I'll go over and see him." With this, Ivan Ivanovich took his stick and his cap and went out to the street. But he had scarcely got through the gate when he remembered the quarrel, spat, and came back.

Almost the same kind of action took place in Ivan Nikiforovich's yard. The old woman, as Ivan Ivanovich noticed, had already put one foot on the wattle fence with the intention of crawling over into his yard, when Ivan Nikiforovich's voice was suddenly heard: "Come back! Come back! You mustn't!"

Ivan Ivanovich became very bored, however; and it is quite likely that these worthy men would have made peace the very next day, if a special occurrence at Ivan Niki-forovich's house had not destroyed all hope and poured oil on the fire of enmity just when it was dying out.

On the evening of that same day, Agafya Fedoseyevna came to visit Ivan Nikiforovich. Agafya Fedoseyevna was neither a relative of Ivan Nikiforovich, nor his sister-in-law, nor even his godmother. Apparently, she had no reason at all for visiting him; and he himself was not too happy to have her there. Nonetheless, she used to come and visit him for weeks on end, and sometimes even longer. When she did, she took possession of the keys and took over the running of the whole house. This was very unpleasant to Ivan Nikiforovich, but surprisingly enough he obeyed her like a child; and although he sometimes tried to argue with her, Agafya Fedoseyevna always won.

I must admit that I don't understand why things are so arranged that women can take us by the nose as deftly as they do the handle of a teapot. Either their hands are just made that way, or our noses aren't better suited for anything else. And despite the fact that Ivan Nikiforovich's nose was quite a bit like a plum, she took him by that nose and led him around like a dog. When she was there, he even altered, unwillingly, his usual mode of life. He didn't lie so long in the sun; and when he did lie there it was not in a state of nature: he always had on his shirt and big, baggy trousers, although Agafya Fedoseyevna by no means insisted on this. She was not one to stand on ceremony, and when Ivan Nikiforovich had a fever she would, with her own hands, rub him down from head to foot with turpentine and vinegar. Agafya Fedoseyevna wore a mob cap on her head, three warts on her nose, and a coffee-coloured housecoat with yellow flowers on it. Her whole figure resembled a tub, so that it was as difficult to locate her waist as to see your own nose without a mirror. Her legs were very short and shaped like two pillows. She talked scandal, ate boiled beets in the morning and swore wonderfully well; and throughout all these varied activities her face did not for a moment change its expression – something which, as a rule, only women can manage.

As soon as she arrived, everything was turned topsy-turvy. "Ivan Nikiforovich, don't you make up with him, and don't apologize. He wants to ruin you – that's the kind of man he is. You don't know him yet."

That damned woman talked slander and more slander, and fixed things so that Ivan Nikiforovich didn't want to hear so much as a mention of Ivan Ivanovich.

Everything took on a different aspect. If a dog from next door ran into the yard, it was drubbed with whatever was handy; those youngsters who crawled across the fence came back howling, with their shabby little shirts pulled up and the marks of a switch on their backs. Even the gaunt old woman, when Ivan Ivanovich tried to ask her about something, made such an indecent gesture that Ivan Ivanovich, as a man of refinement, could only spit and mutter, "What a nasty woman! Worse than her master!"

Finally, to top off all his insults, his hateful neighbour put up – directly opposite his property, at the usual place for climbing over the fence – a goose pen, as though with special intent to aggravate the insult. This shed – so odious to Ivan Ivanovich – was built with diabolical swiftness: in a single day.

This stirred up wrath and a longing for vengeance in Ivan Ivanovich. He did not, however, show any sign of chagrin, although the shed even extended over some of his own land. But his heart beat so hard that it was difficult for him to preserve this outward composure.

Thus did he pass the day. Night came... Oh, if I were a painter, how marvellously would I portray all the loveliness of that night! I would depict all Mirgorod sleeping; the myriad stars looking down on it in stillness; the palpable silence broken by the barking of dogs from nearby and far away; the lovesick sexton hurrying past them and climbing over a fence with knightly intrepidity; the white walls of the houses, bathed in moonlight, becoming still whiter as the trees sheltering them grew darker, the shadows of the trees blacker, the flowers and the silent grass more fragrant, as from every corner the crickets, those indefatigable troubadours of the night, strike up in unison their rasping song. I would depict how, in one of those low-roofed clay cottages, a black-browed village maiden, twisting and turning on her lonely bed, dreams with heaving young breasts of a hussar's moustache and spurs, as the moonlight smiles on her cheeks. I would depict how the black shadow of a bat flits across the white road, as he comes to settle on a white chimney top... But I would scarcely be able to depict Ivan Ivanovich as he went out that night with a saw in his hand. So many different emotions were written on his face! Quietly, very quietly, he crept up and crawled under the goose pen. Ivan Nikiforovich's dogs didn't yet know anything of the quarrel between the two, and they therefore allowed him, as an old acquaintance, to approach the shed, which was supported entirely by four oak posts.

When he had crawled up to the nearest post, he put the saw to it and began sawing. The noise of the sawing made him look around every moment, but the thought of the insult restored his courage.

The first part was sawn through; Ivan Ivanovich began on the second. His eyes were flashing, and he was so terrified he could see nothing. Suddenly, he cried out and went cold all over: a ghost appeared before him. But he soon recovered himself when he saw it was a goose, craning its neck towards him. Ivan Ivanovich spat with indignation and resumed his work.

The second post was likewise sawn through: the goose pen tottered. When he began on the third post his heart was beating so violently that he had to stop his work several times. It was sawn through more than halfway, when the tottering structure gave a sudden, violent lurch... Ivan Ivanovich barely had time to jump out of the way, when it collapsed with a crash. Snatching up his saw, he ran home in a terrible panic and threw himself on his bed, lacking even the courage to look out of the window at the results of his awful deed. It seemed to him that Ivan Nikiforovich's entire household – the old woman, Ivan Nikiforovich, and the small boy in the immense frock coat – had assembled, all of them with clubs and, led by Agafya Fedoseyevna, were coming to tear down his house and smash it to bits.

Ivan Ivanovich passed the whole of the next day as though in a fever. He kept imagining that his fateful neighbour, in revenge for his deed, would at the very least set fire to his house. So he gave orders to Gapka to keep a sharp lookout, everywhere and at every moment, to see whether dry straw hadn't been planted somewhere. At length, in order to forestall Ivan Nikiforovich, he decided to lodge a complaint against him with the Mirgorod District Court. Its contents may be learnt from the following chapter.

Chapter the Fourth

Concerning What Took Place in the
Mirgorod District Court

Mirgorod is a marvellous town! It has all sorts of buildings: some are thatched with straw, some with reeds, and some even have wooden roofs. To the right a street, to the left a street, and everywhere a fine fence. Hops twine over it, pots hang on it, and from behind it the sunflower displays its sunlike head, the poppy blushes, and fat pumpkins can be glimpsed... Splendour! The fence is always adorned with objects that render it still more picturesque: either a checked woollen petticoat spread out wide, or an undershirt, or else a pair of big, baggy trousers. In Mirgorod there is no stealing or misappropriation, so everyone hangs out whatever he wants to.

If you come to the square you will no doubt pause to admire the view. There is a puddle in it – an amazing puddle! The only one like it you ever saw! It covers almost the entire square. A beautiful puddle! The houses and cottages, which from a distance might be taken for haystacks, stand around it admiring its beauty.

But in my opinion there is no finer building than the district courthouse. Whether it is constructed of oak or birchwood is quite unimportant to me; but, my dear sirs, it has eight windows! Eight windows all in a row, looking directly out on the square and upon that body of water I have already mentioned, which the mayor calls a lake! It alone is painted the colour of granite; all the other houses in Mirgorod are merely whitewashed. Its roof is all wood, and it would even have been painted red if the oil intended for that purpose, after having been seasoned with onions, had not been eaten by the office clerks (which happened, as luck would have it, during Lent), so the roof was left unpainted. On the front steps, which project out onto the square, hens often run about, since the steps are almost always littered with grain or some other edibles – which is not done on purpose, however, but only through the carelessness of the petitioners. The courthouse is divided into two parts: in one is the court proper, and in the other is the jail. In the court half there are two clean, white-washed rooms: one is the waiting room for petitioners; the other contains a table adorned with ink stains, and on it stands the *zertsalo.** Four oak chairs with high backs; along the walls, iron-bound chests in which stacks of complaints filed with the district court are kept. On one of the chests, at the moment, a polished boot was standing. The court had been in session since early that morning. The judge, a rather fat man (although somewhat thinner than Ivan Nikiforovich) with a good-natured face, wear-ing a greasy dressing gown, was chatting over a pipe and a cup of tea with his clerk. The judge's lips were located directly under his nose, so that he could sniff his upper lip to his heart's content. This lip served him in lieu of a snuffbox, since the tobacco intended for his nose almost always settled on it. And so, the judge was chatting with his clerk. Off to one side, a barefoot girl was holding a tray of teacups. At the end of the table, the secretary was reading a decision, but in such a monotonous and mournful voice that the defendant himself would have fallen asleep listening to it. The judge would no doubt have done so before anyone else, if he hadn't become involved in an interesting conversation.

"I purposely tried to find out," he was saying, as he sipped from a cup of tea already grown cold, "what they do to make them sing well. I had a wonderful thrush two years ago. And do you know, he suddenly cracked up and began to sing God only knows what. The longer it went on, the worse it got. He started lisping and wheezing – seemed like a hopeless case. But it was a mere nothing. Here's why it happens. Under the throat there's a little lump smaller than a pea. All you have to do is prick that little lump with a needle. Zakhar Prokofyevich showed me how to do it, and if you like I'll tell you just how it happened. I went to his place one day—"

"Shall I read the next one, Demyan Demyanovich?" interrupted the secretary, who had finished reading several minutes before.

"Ah, have you read the whole thing already? My, how fast it went! I didn't hear a bit of it. Where is it? Give it here, and I'll sign it. What else do you have there?"

"The case of the Cossack Bokitko's stolen cow."

"Very well, read it. And so, I went to his place... I can even tell you in detail what he gave me to eat and drink. With the vodka they served sturgeon – unique! I'll tell you, it was nothing at all like the sturgeon" – at this point the judge clicked his tongue and smiled, and his nose sniffed from its usual snuffbox – "that our Mirgorod store treats us to. I didn't eat any herring, because as you know they give me heartburn. But I tasted the caviar. Marvellous

46

caviar! No two ways about it – just marvellous! Then I had some peach brandy distilled with centaury. There was saffron brandy too; but as you know, I never drink it. It's very nice, I realize. Before a meal, they say, it whets your appetite, and afterwards it adds the finishing touch... Well, just look who's here!" exclaimed the judge, seeing Ivan Ivanovich come in.

"God's blessing, and I wish you good health," said Ivan Ivanovich, bowing all around with that amiability which was his and his alone. Lord, how he could charm us all with his manners! I have never seen such refinement anywhere. He was well aware of his own worthiness, and therefore looked upon our unanimous respect as his due. The judge himself offered a chair to Ivan Ivanovich, and his nose sucked up all the snuff from his upper lip – which with him was always a sign of great pleasure.

"What may I offer you, Ivan Ivanovich?" he asked. "Would you like a cup of tea?"

"No, thank you very much," answered Ivan Ivanovich; and he bowed and sat down.

"Oh, please have just one little cup," the judge repeated.

"No, thank you. Very much appreciate your hospitality," answered Ivan Ivanovich. He bowed and sat down.

"Just one cup," repeated the judge.

"No, don't trouble yourself, Demyan Demyanovich." Ivan Ivanovich bowed and sat down.

"One little cup?"

"Well, all right, perhaps one little cup," said Ivan Ivanovich, and reached for the tray.

Merciful Heavens! What boundless refinement there was in that man! Words cannot express what a pleasant impression such manners produce.

"Won't you have another little cup?"

"No, thank you very much," answered Ivan Ivanovich, putting his inverted teacup back on the tray and bowing.

"Do me the favour, Ivan Ivanovich."

"I can't. Much obliged to you." With this, Ivan Ivanovich bowed and sat down.

"Ivan Ivanovich! For our friendship's sake – one little cup!"

"No, thank you. Much indebted to you for your hospitality." Having said this, Ivan Ivanovich bowed and sat down.

"One cup – just one little cup!"

Ivan Ivanovich reached over to the tray and took the cup.

Damn it all, anyway! How does he manage? How does the man keep up his dignity like that?

"Demyan Demyanovich," said Ivan Ivanovich, when he had drunk the last drop, "I have urgent business with you. I am lodging a complaint." With this, Ivan Ivanovich put down his cup and took out of his pocket a sheet of stamped paper covered with writing. "A complaint against my enemy – my sworn enemy."

"But against whom?"

"Against Ivan Nikiforovich Dovgochkhun."

At these words the judge almost fell out of his chair. "What are you saying?" he exclaimed, clasping his hands. "Ivan Ivanovich – is this you?"

"You can see for yourself it is I."

"The Lord and all the holy saints have mercy on us! *What?* You, Ivan Ivanovich, have become the enemy of Ivan Nikiforovich? Did those words come from your lips? Repeat that! Wasn't there someone hiding behind you and speaking instead of you?"

"What's so incredible about it? I can't bear the sight of him. He has offended me mortally. He has defiled my honour."

"By the Holy Trinity! How can I ever make my mother believe this? The dear old thing – every day, as soon as I start quarrelling with my sister, she says, 'Children, you get along like cats and dogs! Why don't you take an example from Ivan Ivanovich and Ivan Nikiforovich? They're real, honest-to-goodness friends! Such friends! Such worthy men!' Some friends, I'll say! Tell me, what's this all about? What happened?"

"It's a delicate matter, Demyan Demyanovich. I can't tell you in so many words. You'd better have your secretary read my petition. Here, take it by this side. It's more presentable here."

"Read it, Taras Tikhonovich," the judge said, turning to his secretary.

Taras Tikhonovich took the petition and, blowing his nose as all secretaries of district courts do – that is, with two fingers – he began to read:

"From Ivan, son of Ivan, Pererepenko, gentleman and landowner of the Mirgorod District, a petition, the substance of which is set forth in the following charges:

1) The gentleman Ivan, son of Nikifor, who is known to the whole world for his ungodly, disgusting and totally unconscionable illegal acts, did, on the seventh day of July of the present year 1810, perpetrate a mortal insult upon me, both personally as affecting my honour and likewise to the degradation and defamation of my rank and family name. The aforesaid gentleman, who is moreover of loathsome appearance, has a quarrelsome

*character and overflows with all manner of blasphe-
mous and abusive expressions..."*

At this point, the secretary paused so as to blow his nose
again, as the judge reverentially folded his arms and just
said to himself: "What a lively pen! Lord, how the man
can write!"

Ivan Ivanovich asked Taras Tikhonovich to read on,
and the latter continued:

*"The aforesaid gentleman Ivan, son of Nikifor,
Dovgochkhun, when I went to him with friendly pro-
posals, called me publicly by an insulting name which
is demeaning to my honour; to wit, "goose"; whereas
it is well known to the entire Mirgorod District that I
have never borne the name of that loathsome animal,
and have no intention of bearing it in the future. The
proof, moreover, of my noble extraction is the fact that
both the day of my birth and the name I received at
baptism are recorded in the parish register kept in the
Church of the Three Bishops. But a goose, as is known
to everyone at all versed in the sciences, cannot be listed
in the parish register, since a goose is not a person but
a fowl – something well known to everyone, even to
a person who has not attended a seminary. But the
aforesaid evil-minded gentleman, being duly aware of
all this, abused me with the aforesaid loathsome word
for no other purpose than to inflict a mortal insult upon
my rank and station.*

*2) This same lewd and indecent gentleman attempted,
moreover, to encroach upon my family property, inherited by me from my father of blessed memory, Ivan,*

son of Onisy, Pererepenko, by profession a member of the clergy, inasmuch as in violation of every law he transported to a point directly opposite my front porch a goose pen; which was done with no other intent than to aggravate the insult perpetrated upon me; for said goose pen had theretofore stood in a very suitable place, and was still reasonably solid. But the abominable intent of the aforementioned gentleman was solely to cause me to witness unseemly incidents; for it is well known that no man goes into a pen – and a fortiori *a goose pen – for any proper purpose. In the course of this illegal action, the two front posts trespassed upon my own land – conveyed to me during the lifetime of my father, Ivan of blessed memory, son of Onisy, Pererepenko, starting from the granary and running in a straight line to the place where the women wash their pots.*

3) The above-described gentleman, whose very names, both first and last, inspire total disgust, nurtures in his heart the evil design of setting fire to me in my own house. Unmistakable indications thereof are manifest from the following: primo, *the aforesaid evil-minded gentleman has begun frequently to emerge from his house – something he never undertook before, owing to his laziness and the loathsome obesity of his body;* secundo, *in his servants' quarters, contiguous to the very fence which forms the boundary of my own land, inherited by me from my late father, Ivan of blessed memory, son of Onisy, Pererepenko, there is a light burning every day and for an unusually long time; which is manifest proof thereof, since hitherto, by reason of his miserly stinginess, not only the tallow candle but also the oil lamp was always put out.*

51

And I therefore petition that the aforesaid gentleman, Ivan, son of Nikifor, Dovgochkhun, as guilty of arson, of the defamation of my rank, Christian name and surname, and of rapacious misappropriation of property – but, above all, of the base and reprehensible coupling of my surname with the appellation of "goose" – be sentenced to the payment of a fine, together with all costs and damages, and that he himself, as a lawbreaker, be put into irons and, when fettered, be sent to the city jail, and that a ruling on this my petition be made promptly and without fail. Written and composed by Ivan, son of Ivan, Pererepenko, gentleman and landowner of Mirgorod."

When the reading of the petition was concluded, the judge went up to Ivan Ivanovich, buttonholed him, and began to speak after this fashion: "What are you doing, Ivan Ivanovich? Fear God! Drop that complaint! Plague take it! (May it dream of the Devil!) Much better you and Ivan Nikiforovich should shake hands, kiss, and make up, and buy some Santorini or Nikopol wine – or else simply make some punch – and invite me. We'll down a bottle together, and forget the whole thing."

"No, Demyan Demyanovich, it's not that kind of thing," said Ivan Ivanovich, with the dignity that always sat so well on him. "It's not the kind of thing that can be settled by a friendly agreement. Goodbye. Goodbye to you, too, gentlemen!" he added, with the same dignity, turning to all the rest of them. "I hope that my petition will bring about appropriate action." And he went out, leaving the whole court dumbfounded.

The judge sat there without saying a word; the secretary took a pinch of snuff; the office clerks upset the shard of a bottle that they used in lieu of an inkwell; and the judge himself, in his distraught condition, spread the puddle of ink over the table with his finger.

"What do you say to that, Dorofei Trofimovich?" asked the judge, turning after a brief silence to his clerk.

"I say nothing," replied the clerk.

"What won't people do next!" the judge went on.

He had scarcely said this, when the door creaked and the front half of Ivan Nikiforovich landed in the courtroom while the other half remained in the waiting room. That Ivan Nikiforovich should appear – and in the courtroom at that – seemed a thing so extraordinary that the judge cried out, and the secretary stopped reading. One clerk, wearing a frieze facsimile of a frock coat, put his pen in his mouth; another swallowed a fly. Even the army veteran who performed the duties of messenger and porter, and who had been standing by the door scratching himself, under his dirty shirt with the stripes on the shoulder – even he gaped and stepped on somebody's foot.

"Well I never! What brought you here? How are you, Ivan Nikiforovich?"

But Ivan Nikiforovich was more dead than alive, because he was stuck fast in the doorway and couldn't take one step either forwards or backwards. In vain did the judge shout into the waiting room that somebody there should shove Ivan Nikiforovich from behind into the courtroom. There was nobody there but an old woman petitioner who, despite all the efforts of her bony hands, could do nothing. Then one of the clerks, who had thick lips, broad shoulders, a thick nose, drunken, crossed eyes and tattered elbows, went up to the front half of Ivan Nikiforovich, folded his arms on his chest as if he were a baby, and winked to the old veteran, who shoved his knee into Ivan Nikiforovich's belly; and in spite of his piteous moans he was squeezed out into the waiting room. Then they slid back the bolts and opened the other half of the door. Meanwhile, the clerk and his assistant, the veteran, breathing hard from their joint efforts, diffused such a strong smell that for a long time the courtroom seemed transformed into a pothouse.

"Are you hurt, Ivan Nikiforovich? I'll tell my mother, and she'll send you a lotion. You just rub it on the small of your back and everything will be all right."

But Ivan Nikiforovich collapsed into a chair, and except for prolonged groans could say nothing. At length, in a faint voice, scarcely audible from exhaustion, he said, "Would you like some?" And taking his snuff horn from his pocket, he added: "Take some! Do me the favour."

"Delighted to see you," answered the judge. "But I still can't imagine what made you take all this trouble and oblige us with such a pleasant surprise."

"A petition..." was all Ivan Nikiforovich could enunciate.

"A petition? What kind of petition?"

"A complaint..." At this point there was a long pause for breath. "...Oof! A complaint against that scoundrel, Ivan Ivanovich Pererepenko!"

"Good Heavens! Are you at it too? Such rare friends! A complaint against such a virtuous man!"

"He's Satan in person!" Ivan Nikiforovich said sharply.

The judge crossed himself.

"Take my petition and read it."

"There's nothing else we can do – read it, Taras Tikhonovich," said the judge, turning to the secretary with an expression of displeasure. But his nose involuntarily sniffed his upper lip, which before then it had usually done only from deep satisfaction. Such self-assertiveness on the part of his nose caused the judge even greater vexation. He took out his handkerchief and wiped all the snuff from his upper lip by way of chastising such insolence.

The secretary, after making the habitual gesture that he always went through before starting to read – without the help of a handkerchief, that is – began in his usual voice as follows:

"The petition of Ivan, son of Nikifor, Dovgochkhun, gentleman of the Mirgorod District, the substance of which is set forth in the following charges:

1) Out of his hateful spite and evident ill will the self-styled gentleman, Ivan, son of Ivan, Pererepenko, is perpetrating against me all manner of dirty tricks, injuries and other evil and dreadful actions; and yesterday p.m., like a robber and a thief, with axes, saws, chisels and other carpenter's tools, he broke at night into my yard and into my own shed, situated therein. With his own hand, and in a humiliating manner, he hacked it to pieces, although I on my part had given no cause for such an illegal and piratical deed.

2) The aforesaid gentleman, Pererepenko, has designs upon my very life, and before the seventh day of last month, concealing those designs, he came to me and began in a friendly and sly manner to wheedle from me

*a shotgun which was in my room, and with his char-
acteristic stinginess offered me many worthless things
for it, such as a brown sow and two sacks of oats. But,
having by then surmised his criminal intent, I tried
in every way to divert him from it; but the aforesaid
scoundrel and villain, Ivan, son of Ivan, Pererepenko,
swore at me like a muzhik, and since that time has
nurtured an implacable hostility towards me. Moreover,
the aforesaid, frequently mentioned ferocious gentleman
and bandit, Ivan, son of Ivan, Pererepenko, is of very
disgraceful origins: his sister was known to all the world
as a slut; she went off with the light-infantry company
stationed in Mirgorod five years ago, and registered her
husband as a peasant. His father and mother were also
exceedingly lawless people, and both were prodigious
drunkards. But the aforementioned gentleman and bandit, Pererepenko, has surpassed all his family with his
brutish and reprehensible behaviour, and under a show
of piety he commits the most immoral acts. He does
not keep the fasts; for on the eve of the fast of Advent,
that godless man bought a ram, and the next day he
ordered his common-law trollop, Gapka, to slaughter
it, alleging that he urgently needed tallow for candles
and oil lamps.*

*Wherefore I petition that the aforesaid gentleman,
as a bandit, sacrilegist and swindler who has already
been detected in theft and burglary, be put into irons
and sent to jail or to a government prison, and there,
as may seem best, having been stripped of his rank
and nobility, be soundly flogged and sent to a penal
camp in Siberia for as long as is necessary; that he be
ordered to pay all costs and damages; and that a ruling*

be made on this my petition. To this petition Ivan, son of Nikifor, Dovgochkhun, gentleman of the Mirgorod District, has set his hand."

As soon as the secretary finished reading, Ivan Nikiforovich picked up his hat and bowed, with the intention of leaving.

"I say, where are you going, Ivan Nikiforovich?" the judge called after him. "Sit with us for a little! Have some tea! Oryshko! Why are you standing there winking at the clerks, foolish girl? Go and bring some tea!"

But Ivan Nikiforovich, terrified at having gone so far away from home and having endured such a dangerous quarantine, had already managed to squeeze through the door, saying, "Don't inconvenience yourself. I'll gladly..." And he closed the door behind him, leaving the whole court dumbfounded.

There was nothing to be done about it. Both complaints were entered, and the case was in the way of assuming considerable importance, when an unforeseen circumstance made it even more interesting. When the judge had left the courtroom, accompanied by his clerk, and the secretary and the office clerks were loading into a sack the chickens, eggs, loaves, pies, cakes and other odds and ends brought by petitioners, a brown sow ran into the room and seized, to the amazement of all present, not a pie or a crust of bread, but Ivan Nikiforovich's petition, which was lying at one end of the table with its pages hanging over the edge. When she had seized the document, the brown grunter ran off so quickly that not one of the clerks could catch her, in spite of the rulers and inkwells that were thrown at her.

This event caused a terrible hubbub, since not so much as one copy of the document had been made. The judge – or rather, his secretary and his clerk – spent a long time discussing this unprecedented development. Finally, it was decided to write a report on it for the mayor, since the investigation of this case was more the concern of the police. The report, No. 389, was sent to him that same day, and out of it grew a rather curious conversation, about which the reader may learn in the following chapter.

Chapter the Fifth

*In Which Is Described a Conference between Two
Eminent Personages of Mirgorod*

N O SOONER HAD Ivan Ivanovich taken care of things
on his property and gone out, as usual, to lie on the
porch than, to his unutterable astonishment, he noticed
something red at the front gate. This was the mayor's red
cuff, which like his collar had acquired a glaze, and along
the edges was being transformed into polished leather.
Ivan Ivanovich thought to himself: "I'm really pleased
that Pyotr Fyodorovich has come for a chat." But he was
very surprised to see that the mayor was walking much
faster than usual and waving his hands – which as a rule
he did very rarely. There were eight buttons on the mayor's
uniform. The ninth had come off during a procession at
the consecration of the church two years before, and so
far the police force had not managed to find it, although
the mayor, when hearing the daily reports made to him
by the inspectors, always asked whether the button had
been found. These eight buttons were sewn on the way
peasant women plant beans: one to the right, and the
next to the left. His left leg had taken a bullet in his last
campaign, so that as he limped along, he threw it out so
far to the side that he thereby nullified almost all the work
of the right leg. The more rapidly the mayor manoeuvred

his infantry, the slower it advanced. Thus, while he was approaching the porch, Ivan Ivanovich had time enough to lose himself in conjectures as to why the mayor was waving his arms so fast. He was all the more interested because the business at hand was apparently of unusual importance, since the mayor was even wearing his new sword.

"Hello, Pyotr Fyodorovich!" called out Ivan Ivanovich, who, as has already been said, was most inquisitive and simply could not restrain his impatience at the sight of the mayor trying to take the porch steps by storm without raising his eyes as he quarrelled with his infantry, which was quite unable to mount the step at one fell swoop.

"A very good day to you, my dear friend and benefactor Ivan Ivanovich!" answered the mayor.

"Pray sit down. You're tired. I can see that, because your wounded leg hinders—"

"My leg!" cried the mayor, giving Ivan Ivanovich one of those looks such as a giant casts at a pygmy, or a learned pedant at a dancing master. As he said this, he stretched out his leg and stamped on the floor. This valour, however, cost him dear, because his whole body lurched forward and his nose pecked at the railing. But the sage guardian of law and order, by way of saving face, at once righted himself and reached into his pocket as though trying to get at his snuffbox. "Let me tell you, my very dear friend and benefactor Ivan Ivanovich, that I've made much worse campaigns in my day. Yes, seriously, I have. In the campaign of 1807, for instance… Oh, I could tell you how I climbed over a fence to visit a pretty German girl." With this, the mayor winked, and smiled a fiend-ishly roguish smile.

"But where have you been today?" asked Ivan Ivanovich, eager to cut the mayor short and bring him more quickly to the reason for his visit. He would very much have liked to ask what it was the mayor intended to inform him of. But his refined social awareness made him realize how very improper such a question would be; and he had to control himself and wait for the key to the riddle, although meanwhile his heart was pounding with unusual violence.

"Very well, I'll tell you where I've been," the mayor answered. "In the first place, I report that the weather is fine today."

At these words, Ivan Ivanovich almost died.

"But allow me," the mayor continued. "I came to see you today about a very important matter." With this, the mayor's face and bearing took on the same anxious aspect they had had when he was storming the porch.

Ivan Ivanovich came alive again, and shook as though in a fever; but, as usual, he was not long in asking a question.

"How is it important? Is it really important?"

"Well, judge for yourself. First of all, I beg to inform you, dear friend and benefactor Ivan Ivanovich, that you... for my part, mind you, I don't care at all; but the policy of the government demands it... you have committed a breach of public order!"

"What are you saying, Pyotr Fyodorovich? I don't understand it at all."

"I swear, Ivan Ivanovich! How can you say you don't understand it at all? Your own beast has made off with a very important official document, and you still say you can't understand it at all!"

"What beast?"

"If I may say so, your own brown sow."

"But how is it my fault? Why did the court porter open the door?"

"But, Ivan Ivanovich, the beast was your own, so you are to blame."

"Thank you very much for putting me on the same level with a pig."

"I never said that, Ivan Ivanovich! As God is my judge, I never said that! Kindly judge for yourself with an open mind. You are beyond any doubt aware that, in accordance with the policy of the government, unclean beasts are prohibited from straying about in the town – especially in the main streets. You must admit that this is prohibited."

"Good Lord, what are you talking about? What difference does it make if a hog goes out in the street?"

"Allow me to inform you – allow me, Ivan Ivanovich – that this is quite impossible. What can we do? If our superiors want something, we must obey. I don't deny that chickens and geese sometimes run out into the street, and even the square. Chickens and geese, mind you. But already last year I issued an order that hogs and goats were not to be allowed in public places. Which order I commanded to be read aloud at that time before an assembly of all the townspeople."

"Pyotr Fyodorovich, I see nothing in all this except that you are trying in every way to offend me."

"That's one thing you simply can't say, my very dear friend and benefactor – that I'm trying to offend you. Just try to remember: I didn't say a word to you last year when you put up a roof a whole yard higher than what regulations permit. On the contrary, I pretended I hadn't noticed it at all. Believe me, my very dear friend, even now I would absolutely... er, so to speak... But my duty – in a word, my responsibility – requires me to enforce cleanliness. Judge for yourself, when suddenly, in the main street—"

"Fine main streets they are! Every peasant woman goes there to throw out whatever she doesn't want."

"Permit me to inform you, Ivan Ivanovich, that it's *you* who are offending *me*. True enough – that does happen sometimes, but as a rule only beside a fence, or behind sheds or storehouses. But when a sow in farrow barges into the main street and the public square, that's something—"

"Really now, Pyotr Fyodorovich! After all, a sow is one of God's creatures!"

"Agreed! Everybody knows that you're an educated man – that you know all the sciences and various other subjects. I didn't start learning to write until I was thirty. Because, as you know, I rose from the ranks."

"Hm!" said Ivan Ivanovich.

"Yes," the mayor went on, "in 1801 I was a lieutenant in the 42nd Light Infantry Regiment. Our company commander, if you would care to know, was Captain Yeremeyev." As he said this, the mayor dipped his fingers into the snuffbox that Ivan Ivanovich was proffering, and rolled some snuff between his thumb and forefinger.

Ivan Ivanovich answered, "Hm!"

"But it is my duty," continued the mayor, "to obey the orders of the government. Are you aware, Ivan Ivanovich, that anyone who steals a government document from a courtroom must be tried before a criminal court like any other criminal?"

"I'm so well aware of it that, if you like, I can teach you something. That applies to human beings – if you stole a document, for example. But a pig is an animal – one of God's creatures."

"That's all very well, but the law says: 'Anyone guilty of stealing'... Please listen carefully: '*Anyone* guilty'. Nothing is said about the species, sex or rank. Therefore, an animal can be guilty too. You may think what you please, but the beast, prior to being sentenced, must be turned over to the police as a violator of law and order."

"No, Pyotr Fyodorovich," Ivan Ivanovich replied coolly, "that will not be."

"As you like, but I must follow the orders of the government."

"Why are you trying to frighten me? I suppose you mean to send that one-armed soldier for the sow? I'll tell my serf girl to take a poker to him and throw him out. She'll break his other arm."

"I won't venture to argue with you. If you don't want to turn her over to the police, then do whatever you like with her. Butcher her for Christmas, if you want to, and make hams out of her. Or eat her just as she is. Only if you're going to make sausages, I wish you'd send me a couple of those that your Gapka makes so well out of hog's blood and lard. My Agrafena Trofimovna is very fond of them."

"I'll be delighted to send you a couple of sausages."

"I'll be very much obliged to you, my dear friend and benefactor. Now allow me to say just one more thing. I have been especially asked by both the judge and all of our other acquaintances to – so to speak – reconcile you with your friend, Ivan Nikiforovich."

"*What?* With that boor? You want me to make peace with that coarse individual? Never! That will never be – never!"

"As you like," answered the mayor, regaling both nostrils with snuff. "I won't make so bold as to offer advice. But allow me to point out one thing. Right now you two are at odds; but when you've made up..."

But Ivan Ivanovich had begun to talk about catching quails, which usually happened when he wanted to change the subject.

And so the mayor was obliged to depart without having achieved any success whatsoever.

Chapter the Sixth

From Which the Reader Can Easily Learn
All That Is Contained in It

DESPITE ALL THE EFFORTS made by the court to conceal the matter, the very next day all Mirgorod learnt that Ivan Ivanovich's sow had made off with Ivan Nikiforovich's petition. It was the mayor himself, in a forgetful moment, who was the first to spill the beans. When Ivan Nikiforovich was told of it, he said nothing except to enquire, "Was it the brown one?"

But Agafya Fedoseyevna, who was there at the time, started needling Ivan Nikiforovich again. "What's the matter with you, Ivan Nikiforovich? If you let it pass, people will laugh at you for a fool! A fine gentleman you'll be then! You'll be worse than the woman who sells those pies you're so fond of!"

And that tireless woman talked him around! Somewhere she dug up a little man, middle-aged and swarthy, with blotches all over his face, who wore a dark-blue frock coat with patched elbows – a regular bureaucratic scribbler! He smeared tar on his topboots, had three quill pens stuck behind each ear, and for an inkpot he had a little glass bottle tied to a button by a string. He would eat nine pies at a sitting, and put the tenth in his pocket, and would fill one sheet of stamped foolscap with all manner of chicanery

66

so that no clerk could read it aloud straight through, but would have to pause time and again to cough or sneeze. This little semblance of a man fussed and sweated and scribbled, and finally concocted the following document:

To the Mirgorod District Court from the gentleman Ivan, son of Nikifor, Dovgochkhun.

As a consequence of the aforesaid my petition, which was from me, the gentleman Ivan, son of Nikifor, Dovgochkhun, and so intended, jointly with the gentleman Ivan, son of Ivan, Pererepenko, at which the Mirgorod District Court itself manifested its connivance. And the aforesaid insolent wilfulness of the brown sow being itself kept secret and having reached our ears from persons not party to the case. Forasmuch as the aforesaid indulgence and connivance, as of malicious intent, falls strictly within the competence of the court; for said sow is a stupid beast, and hence all the more capable of stealing official documents. From which it is clearly evident that the frequently aforementioned sow could not but have been incited to the same by the opposing party himself, the self-styled gentleman Ivan, son of Ivan, Pererepenko, who has already been detected in theft, attempted homicide and sacrilege. But the aforesaid Mirgorod Court, with its characteristic partiality, manifested the tacit consent of its own person, without which consent said sow could never have been allowed to abscond with the document; inasmuch as the Mirgorod District Court is well provided with attendants, for which it suffices to mention a certain soldier at all times present in the waiting room who, although he has one blind eye and a somewhat damaged arm, possesses the requisite capacity to drive out a hog and strike it with a cudgel. Wherefrom is abundantly evident the connivance of the aforesaid Mirgorod Court and, incontestably, the sharing of the Jew-like profits therefrom, mutually combining. And the aforesaid, aforementioned bandit and gentleman Ivan, son of Ivan, Pererepenko, who has disgraced himself, was the accomplice. Wherefore I, the gentleman Ivan, son of Nikifor, Dovgochkhun, herewith inform the aforesaid District Court in its appropriate omniscience that if the aforementioned petition is not recovered from said brown sow or from her accomplice, the gentleman Pererepenko, and a just ruling in my favour is not made thereupon, then I, Ivan, son of Nikifor, Dovgochkhun, will lodge a complaint with the higher court regarding such illegal connivance of the aforesaid District Court, with due and appropriate transference of the case.

— Ivan, son of Nikifor, Dovgochkhun, gentleman of the Mirgorod District.

This petition produced its effect. The judge, like all kind-hearted people, was a cowardly man. He asked the secretary for his opinion. But the secretary emitted a deep "Hm" through his lips, and his face took on the indifferent and diabolically ambiguous expression that is assumed only by Satan when he sees at his feet the victim who has run to him for help. One recourse was left: to reconcile the two friends. But how to go about this, when so far all attempts had been unsuccessful? Nonetheless, they decided to try. But Ivan Ivanovich declared flatly that he would have none of it, and even got very angry. Ivan Nikiforovich, instead of answering, turned his back to

the sun and didn't say a word. Then the litigation pro-
ceeded with the extraordinary rapidity for which the
mills of justice are ordinarily so famed. The document
was earmarked, registered, numbered, sewn into a paper
case, and receipted for – all in one day; and the paper
case was put on a shelf, where it lay and lay and lay – for
one year, then another, and another. A great many young
ladies managed to get married; a new street was built in
Mirgorod; the judge lost one molar and two side teeth;
more urchins were running about Ivan Ivanovich's yard
than before (Lord only knows where they came from);
Ivan Nikiforovich, by way of reproaching Ivan Ivanovich,
had built a new goose pen, although somewhat farther
away than the former one, and had put up enough other
outbuildings to screen himself off completely from Ivan
Ivanovich, so that these worthy men almost never saw
each other face to face – and the case still lay, in perfect
order, there on the shelf, which had turned marble-like
from the ink stains.

Meanwhile, an event of great importance to all Mirgorod took place.

The mayor was giving a party! Where shall I find brushes
and colours to paint the variety of the gathering and the
magnificent revelry? Take a watch, open it up, and look
at what's going on inside. A frightful hotchpotch, is it
not? Now just imagine that almost as many, if not more,
wheels were standing in the mayor's yard. What britzkas
and springless carriages were not there! One with a broad
rear end and a narrow front; another with a narrow rear
end and a broad front. One was a britzka and a springless
carriage combined; another was neither a britzka nor a
springless carriage; and another was like a huge haystack

or a fat merchant's wife; another was like a dishevelled Jew or a skeleton that has not yet shed all its skin; another looked, in profile, exactly like a pipe with a long stem; still another like nothing on earth – some kind of strange being utterly hideous and most fantastic. From the midst of this chaos of wheels and coach boxes loomed the semblance of a carriage with a window like that of a room barred with a thick crosspiece. Coachmen in long-waisted grey Cossack coats, tunics and grey jerkins, sheepskin caps, and forage caps of various sizes and shapes, with pipes in their mouths, were leading the unharnessed horses through the yard. What a party the mayor was giving! Permit me to list all those present: Taras Tarasovich, Yevpl Akinfovich, Yevtikhy Yevtikhyevich, Ivan Ivanovich (not our Ivan Ivanovich, but another), Savva Gavrilovich, our Ivan Ivanovich, Yelevfery Yelevferyevich, Makar Nazaryevich, Foma Grigoryevich… I can't go on! My strength fails me! My hand is tired from writing. And how many ladies there were! Swarthy and fair, long and short, some fat as Ivan Nikiforovich, and some so thin it seemed each one of them could be hidden in the scabbard of the mayor's sword. So many bonnets! So many dresses! Red, yellow, coffee-coloured, green, dark-blue; new, turned, remade; headscarves, ribbons, reticules. Farewell, poor eyes! You'll be no good for anything after this spectacle. And what a long table was pulled out! And how everybody talked – what a racket they raised! A mill, with all its grindstones, wheels, pinions and beaters is as nothing compared to that. I can't tell you for sure what they were talking about, but it must have been about many pleasant and useful subjects such as the weather, dogs, wheat, bonnets and stallions. At length Ivan Ivanovich – not our

Ivan Ivanovich, but the one-eyed one – said: "It strikes me as strange that my right eye" (the one-eyed Ivan Ivanovich always spoke of himself ironically) "does not see Ivan Nikiforovich Dovgochkhun."

"He wouldn't come!" said the mayor.

"How so?"

"Well, it's already been two years, thank the Lord, since they quarrelled – I mean Ivan Ivanovich and Ivan Nikiforovich; and if one of them goes somewhere, the other won't go for the life of him."

"You don't say so!" At this, the one-eyed Ivan Ivanovich cast his eyes upwards and clasped his hands. "Well, now, if people with good eyes can't get along together, how can I live in peace with my blind orb?"

At these words everybody laughed heartily. They were all very fond of the one-eyed Ivan Ivanovich, because he cracked jokes very much in the taste of the day. Even the tall, thin man in a soft woollen frock coat with a plaster on his nose, who up to then had been sitting in a corner and never once changed the expression on his face – even that gentleman rose from his seat and came nearer to the crowd that had gathered around the one-eyed Ivan Ivanovich.

"I'll tell you what," said the one-eyed Ivan Ivanovich, when he saw he was surrounded by a rather large company. "Instead of staring at my blind eye, as you are doing now, let's reconcile our two friends. Right now Ivan Ivanovich is chatting with the women and young girls. Let's send on the sly for Ivan Nikiforovich, and then shove them together."

Everyone unanimously adopted Ivan Ivanovich's proposal and decided to send at once to Ivan Nikiforovich's house and beg him to come to the mayor's for dinner at all costs. But the important problem of who was to be entrusted with this important mission threw all of them into a quandary. For a long time they argued about who was most capable and skilful in matters of diplomacy; and finally they decided unanimously to entrust all this to Anton Prokofyevich Golopuz.*

But first we must acquaint the reader a bit with this remarkable person. Anton Prokofyevich was a thoroughly virtuous man in the full meaning of that word. If anyone among the worthy people of Mirgorod gave him a scarf or some underwear, he would thank him. If anyone gave him a slight fillip on the nose, he would thank him too. If he was asked, "Anton Prokofyevich, why is your coat brown while the sleeves are blue?" he would always answer, "You don't even have one! Wait a bit. It will soon get shabby, and then it will be the same all over." And sure enough: the blue cloth began to turn brown from the effect of the sun, and now it is the same colour as the rest of the coat! But what is strange is that Anton Prokofyevich has the habit of wearing woollen clothes in the summer and nankeen in the winter. Anton Prokofyevich doesn't have a house of his own. He used to have one on the edge of town, but he sold it, and with the proceeds he bought three bay horses and a little britzka in which he used to go about visiting the landowners. But since the horses were a lot of trouble, and besides that he needed money to buy oats for them, Anton Prokofyevich traded them for a fiddle and a serf girl, getting a twenty-five-rouble note into the bargain. Then Anton Prokofyevich sold the fiddle and traded the serf girl for a morocco purse set with gold. And now he has a purse the likes of which nobody else has. As a price for this pleasure, he can no longer drive about the countryside, but must stay in town and spend the night at various homes – especially of those gentlemen who have found gratification in filliping him on the nose. Anton Prokofyevich likes to dine well, and plays a rather good game of "Fools" and "Millers".*

Obedience was always a natural thing for him; and so, taking his cap and walking stick, he set off at once. But on the way he began pondering how he could get Ivan Nikiforovich to come to the party. The rather stern disposition of that otherwise estimable man made his task almost impossible. And, in fact, how could he make up his mind to come, when even to get out of bed cost him such great effort? But supposing he did get up, how could he bring himself to go to a place where – as he undoubtedly knew – his irreconcilable enemy was to be found? The more Anton Prokofyevich pondered it, the more obstacles he found. The day was sultry, the sun was scorching, and he was dripping with sweat. Despite the fact that people flicked him on the nose, Anton Prokofyevich was a rather canny fellow in many matters. (It was only in swapping that he was not too lucky.) He knew very well when he had to make himself out a fool; and sometimes he was able to cope in situations and cases wherein an intelligent man is seldom able to keep his head above water.

While his inventive mind was thinking up ways to persuade Ivan Nikiforovich, and while he was going bravely forward to encounter the worst, an unforeseen circumstance somewhat discountenanced him. In this connection it might be well to inform the reader that Anton Prokofyevich had, among other things, a pair of trousers of such a strange description that whenever he put them

73

on the dogs always bit him in the calf of the leg. As ill luck would have it, he had put on those same trousers that day. So that hardly had he plunged into his ponderings, when a terrible barking from all directions assailed his ears. Anton Prokofyevich set up such an outcry – no one could shout louder than he could – that not only our friend the old serving woman and the inhabitant of the immense frock coat ran out to meet him, but even the urchins from Ivan Ivanovich's yard descended upon him; and although the dogs only managed to bite one of his legs, this greatly dampened his spirits, and he went up the porch steps with a certain timidity.

Chapter the Seventh

– and Last

"AH, HOW DO YOU DO? Why were you teasing the dogs?" said Ivan Nikiforovich, when he saw Anton Prokofyevich – since no one ever spoke otherwise than in jest to Anton Prokofyevich.

"A plague on them all! I'm not teasing them!" answered Anton Prokofyevich.

"You're lying!"

"I'm not – I swear it! Pyotr Fyodorovich wants you to come to dinner."

"Hm."

"I swear it! He put it so persuasively – I simply can't tell you. 'Why is it,' says he, 'that Ivan Nikiforovich avoids me like an enemy? He never comes for a chat, or to sit a bit.'"

Ivan Nikiforovich stroked his chin.

"'If Ivan Nikiforovich doesn't come this time,' he says, 'I won't know what to think. Most likely he has some design against me. Do me a favour, Anton Prokofyevich, and persuade Ivan Nikiforovich!' What do you say, Ivan Nikiforovich? Let's go! There's a fine company gathered there now."

Ivan Nikiforovich started to scrutinize a rooster who was standing on the porch steps and crowing with all his might.

"If only you knew, Ivan Nikiforovich," continued the zealous spokesman, "what sturgeon and fresh caviar have been sent to Pyotr Fyodorovich's!"

At those words, Ivan Nikiforovich turned his head and began to listen closely. This encouraged the spokesman.

"Let's get started right now! Foma Grigoryevich is there too. What's the matter?" he added, when he saw that Ivan Nikiforovich was still lying in the same position.

"I don't want to."

This "I don't want to" jolted Anton Prokofyevich. He had been quite sure that his persuasive representations had completely won over this generally worthy man, instead of which he heard a resolute "I don't want to".

"Why don't you want to?" he asked, almost with annoyance – something he displayed very rarely, even when burning paper was put on his head: an amusement that the judge and the mayor were especially fond of.

Ivan Nikiforovich took a pinch of snuff.

"Have it your way, Ivan Nikiforovich. But I really don't know what's preventing you."

"Why should I go?" Ivan Nikiforovich said at last. "That bandit will be there!"

That was what he usually called Ivan Ivanovich. Good Heavens! And not so long ago...

"I swear he won't be there. By all that's holy, he won't! May I be struck dead by a thunderbolt on this very spot!" replied Anton Prokofyevich, who was ready to swear an oath ten times every hour. "Let's go, Ivan Nikiforovich!"

"But you're lying, Anton Prokofyevich. He's there, isn't he?"

"I swear he isn't! I swear it! May I never leave this spot if he is! Judge for yourself. Why should I lie? May my arms and legs wither!... What, you still don't believe me? May I drop dead here at your feet! May neither my father nor my mother nor myself ever see the kingdom of Heaven! Do you still refuse to believe me?"

Ivan Nikiforovich was completely calmed by these assurances, and he ordered his valet in the immense frock coat to bring his big, baggy trousers and his nankeen Cossack coat.

I assume it is quite superfluous to describe how Ivan Nikiforovich put on his big, baggy trousers, how his cravat was tied and, finally, how he was helped on with his Cossack coat, which had burst its seams under the left sleeve. Suffice it to say that during all this time he maintained a decorous composure and did not say one word in answer to Anton Prokofyevich's proposal that he should trade him something for his Turkish purse.

Meanwhile, the assembled guests were impatiently waiting the decisive moment when Ivan Nikiforovich would appear and the universal desire that these two friends should be reconciled might at last be fulfilled. Many of them were almost certain that Ivan Nikiforovich would not come. The mayor even made a bet with the one-eyed Ivan Ivanovich that he wouldn't come; but he gave it up merely because the one-eyed Ivan Ivanovich demanded that the former stake his wounded leg against his own blind eye – at which the mayor took great offence, while the guests laughed on the sly. No one had yet sat down at the table, although it was well past one o'clock – an hour when the people of Mirgorod have usually long been dining, even on gala occasions.

Hardly had Anton Prokofyevich appeared in the doorway, when he was instantly surrounded by everyone. In answer to all questions, he shouted one decisive phrase: "He won't come." He had scarcely said this, and a shower of reproaches and curses and possibly even fillips was about to come down on his head for the failure of his mission, when suddenly the door opened and... in walked Ivan Nikiforovich.

If Satan himself or a corpse had appeared, he would not have caused such amazement to all the assembled guests as that into which they were thrown by the unexpected entrance of Ivan Nikiforovich. As for Anton Prokofyevich, he went off into gales of laughter, holding his sides with glee at having played such a joke on the whole company.

In any case, it seemed almost incredible to everyone that Ivan Nikiforovich had managed, in so short a time, to dress as befits a gentleman. Ivan Ivanovich was not there at that moment; he had gone off somewhere. When they had recovered from their amazement, all the guests showed their interest in Ivan Nikiforovich's health, and said they were glad to see he had grown stouter. Ivan Nikiforovich exchanged kisses with all of them and said, "Much obliged."

Meanwhile the smell of hot borscht drifted through the room and pleasantly tickled the nostrils of the starving guests. They all flocked into the dining room. A line of ladies, talkative and taciturn, fat and thin, filed in ahead, and the long table soon glittered with all possible colours. I am not going to describe all the courses on the table. I will make no mention of the dumplings in sour cream, of the sweetbreads served with the borscht, of the turkey stuffed with plums and raisins, of the course that very much resembled a pair of boots soaked in kvass, nor of that sauce which is the swansong of the ancient cook: that sauce that came to the table enveloped in flaming spirits – which greatly amused the ladies, and at the same time terrified them. I am not going to talk about these dishes because I take much greater pleasure in eating them than in discussing them at length.

Ivan Ivanovich very much enjoyed the fish prepared with horseradish sauce. He devoted himself especially to this useful and nourishing pastime. As he was picking out the smallest fish bones and laying them on his plate, he happened to glance across the table. Great God in heaven, what a strange thing! Across from him sat Ivan Nikiforovich!

At the same time, Ivan Nikiforovich also looked up... No, I'm not equal to it!... Give me another pen. Mine is flabby, dead, with too thin a nib for this scene. Their faces, with amazement reflected on them, seemed petrified. Each of them recognized a long-familiar face – a person to whom, one would have thought, he was instinctively ready to come up as to a friend who had appeared from nowhere, and proffer his snuffbox with the words, "Do me the favour," or, "May I be so bold as to ask you to do me the favour?" But instead of that, the face was frightful, like an evil portent. The sweat poured off both Ivan Ivanovich and Ivan Nikiforovich.

All of the guests at the table were dumbstruck from staring, and none of them could take their eyes off the erstwhile friends. The ladies, who up to that moment

79

had been engaged in a rather interesting discussion about how to prepare capons, suddenly cut their talk short. All was stilled. It was a picture worthy of the brush of a great artist.

At length Ivan Ivanovich took out his handkerchief and began to blow his nose; meanwhile, Ivan Nikiforovich looked about him and fixed his eyes on the open door. The mayor immediately noticed this movement, and ordered the door closed tight. Then both of the friends began to eat, and did not look up at each other again.

The moment dinner was over, both former friends rose from their seats and began looking for their caps so they could slip away. At this point, the mayor winked, and Ivan Ivanovich – not our Ivan Ivanovich, but the one-eyed one – got behind Ivan Nikiforovich, while the mayor got behind Ivan Ivanovich, and both began shoving them from behind so as to push them together and not let them go until they had shaken hands. Ivan Ivanovich – the one-eyed one – pushed Ivan Nikiforovich, somewhat indirectly but nonetheless rather successfully, to the place where Ivan Ivanovich was standing. But the mayor got way off course, since he could in no wise cope with his headstrong infantry, which this time obeyed no commands whatsoever and, as though to spite him, swung itself exceedingly far off in the opposite direction (which might very well have been due to the fact that there were a great many different liqueurs on the table after dinner), so that Ivan Ivanovich fell on a lady in a red dress who, out of curiosity, had thrown herself into the very midst of things. This omen boded no good. The judge, however, set things to rights, took the mayor's place and, after sniffing up all the tobacco from his upper lip, shoved Ivan Ivanovich in the other direction. In Mirgorod, this is the customary procedure for peacemaking. It is rather like a game of catch with a ball. As soon as the judge had shoved Ivan Ivanovich, Ivan Ivanovich – the one-eyed one – laid on with all his strength and shoved Ivan Nikiforovich, from whom the sweat was pouring like rainwater from a roof. Both friends resisted stoutly, but they were brought together anyway, since both of the active parties received considerable support from the other guests.

Then they were closely hemmed in on all sides, and were not let go until they had made up their minds to shake hands.

"For Heaven's sake, Ivan Ivanovich and Ivan Nikiforovich! Tell us in all honesty: what were you quarrelling about? Wasn't it over a mere nothing? Aren't you ashamed before men and before God?"

"I don't know," said Ivan Nikiforovich, panting with exhaustion (it was obvious that he was not at all opposed to a reconciliation). "I don't know what I did to Ivan Ivanovich. But why did he saw down my goose pen and plot to destroy me?"

"I'm innocent of any evil designs," said Ivan Ivanovich, not looking at Ivan Nikiforovich. "I swear before God and before you, worthy gentlemen, that I did nothing to my enemy. Why, then, does he revile me and defame my rank and title?"

"How did I defame you, Ivan Ivanovich?" said Ivan Nikiforovich.

One more minute of explanation, and the long-standing feud would have been on the point of extinction. Ivan

Nikiforovich had already reached into his pocket to get out his snuff horn and say, "Do me the favour."

"Was it not defamation," replied Ivan Ivanovich without raising his eyes, "when you, sir, insulted my rank and family name with a word which it would be unseemly to utter here?"

"Allow me to tell you as friend to friend, Ivan Ivanovich" (as he said this, Ivan Nikiforovich touched a finger to a buttonhole of Ivan Ivanovich's, which showed his completely favourable inclination) "that you took offence at the Devil only knows what. Just because I called you a *goose*."

Ivan Nikiforovich realized immediately that he had been careless in uttering that word, but it was already too late: the word had been uttered.

Everything went to the Devil.

If, when that word was uttered with no witnesses present, Ivan Ivanovich lost all self-control and flew into such a rage as God grant a person may never behold, then what now? Only judge for yourselves, gentle readers. What now, when that deadly word was uttered in an assemblage including large numbers of the fair sex, in whose presence Ivan Ivanovich liked to be especially proper? If Ivan Nikiforovich had behaved in any other way – if he had said "fowl" instead of "goose"? The situation could still have been saved.

But it was all over and finished...

Ivan Ivanovich threw a look at Ivan Nikiforovich – and what a look! If that look had been endowed with effective power, Ivan Nikiforovich would have been reduced to ashes. The guests understood that look and hastened to separate them. And this man, the very model of gentleness, who never let a single beggar woman pass by without questioning her, rushed out in a terrible rage. Such violent storms do the passions produce!

For a whole month nothing was heard of Ivan Ivanovich. He locked himself in his house. His ancestral trunk was opened, and from that trunk were removed... what? Silver roubles! His grandfather's old silver roubles. And those roubles passed into the soiled hands of shyster lawyers. The case was transferred to the higher court. And it was only when Ivan Ivanovich received the joyful news that it would be settled the following day, that he looked out upon the world and decided to emerge from his house. Alas! From that time onward, for the next ten years, the higher court notified him daily that the case would be settled the next day.

Five years ago I passed through the town of Mirgorod. I was travelling in a poor time of the year. It was autumn, with its cheerlessly damp weather, mud and mist. A kind of unnatural verdure – the work of dreary, incessant rains – had spread its insubstantial network over the meadows and grain fields, to which it was as becoming as a prank to an old man or a rose to an old woman. In those days, the weather had a powerful influence on me: when it was dreary, I felt dreary. But in spite of that, when I began to draw near to Mirgorod I felt my heart beating violently. Lord, how many memories! I hadn't seen Mirgorod for twelve years. Back then, two unique persons, two unique friends, had lived here in touching friendship. And how many eminent men had died! Judge Demyan Demyanovich had already passed away, and Ivan Ivanovich – the one-eyed one – had also departed this life.

I drove into the main street. Everywhere stood poles with wisps of straw tied to the top: some new kind of surveying work was in progress. Several cottages had been torn down. The remnants of wooden and wattle fences stood there looking sad.

It was a holiday. I ordered my kibitka to stop in front of the church, and entered so quietly that no one turned around. Truth to tell, there was no one to do so. The church was empty – almost nobody there. Plainly, even the most devout worshipers were afraid of the mud. On this overcast – or, rather, sickly – day, the candles were strangely unpleasant, somehow; the darkened front part of the church was saddening; and the oblong windows with their round panes were streaming with tears of rain.

I walked into the front part of the church and addressed a venerable old man with grey hair. "Tell me, please. Is Ivan Nikiforovich still alive?"

Just then the lamp in front of an icon flared up, and the light fell directly on his face. How surprised I was when I looked at him closely and recognized the familiar features. It was Ivan Nikiforovich himself! But how he had changed!

"Are you well, Ivan Nikiforovich? How you have aged!"

"Yes, I've aged. I'm just back from Poltava today," answered Ivan Nikiforovich.

"*What?* You went to Poltava in this dreadful weather?"

"I had no choice. My lawsuit…"

At this I couldn't help sighing. Ivan Nikiforovich noticed my sigh, and said, "Don't worry. I have reliable information that the case will be decided next week – and in my favour."

I shrugged my shoulders and went to find out something about Ivan Ivanovich.

"Ivan Ivanovich is here!" someone told me. "He's in the choir loft."

Then I noticed a gaunt form. Was this Ivan Ivanovich? His face was all wrinkles, and his hair was completely white; but his fitted coat was still the same. After the first greetings, Ivan Ivanovich, having given me that cheerful smile which went so well with his funnel-shaped face, said, "May I tell you some good news?"

"What news?" I asked.

"My case will be decided tomorrow without fail. The high court has said so for certain."

I sighed even more deeply, made haste to say goodbye (since I was travelling on very important business), and got into my kibitka. The skinny horses, known in Mirgorod as post-horses, started off, producing with their hoofs, which had sunk into the grey mud, a sound that was unpleasant to the ear. The rain came down in torrents on the Jew sitting on the coach box, who had covered himself with matting. The dampness went all the way through me. The town gate, with a sentry box in which an old soldier was repairing his grey implements, passed slowly by. Again the same fields, ploughed and black in some places, and green in others, the wet jackdaws and crows, the monotonous rain, the tearful sky without a streak of light. It is dreary in this world, gentlemen!

1834

A Panegyric in Memory of My Grandfather

*Delivered by a Friend to an Audience
of His Friends, over a Bowl of Punch*

Ivan Krylov

DEAR FRIENDS! THIS DAY marks the passing of exactly one year since the dogs of this world lost their best friend, and our district its wisest landowner. One year ago, to the very day, while intrepidly pursuing a hare, he fell in a ditch and shared the fatal cup, most fraternally, with his bay horse. Fate, respecting their mutual affection, did not want either of them to outlive the other. Meanwhile, the world lost its finest gentleman and its handsomest horse. Which of the two is the more deserving of our sorrow? Of our praise? In the matter of virtues, neither was second to the other. Both were equally useful to society; both led the same kind of life; and, finally, both died the same glorious death.

Still, my friendship for the departed inclines me in his favour and obliges me to glorify his memory. For, though many may say that his heart was (so to speak) the stable of his bay horse, I may flatter myself that next to her, he loved me better than anything else on earth. But even if he had not been my friend, would not his sterling qualities merit praise for themselves alone? And should not his memory be exalted as one which will serve as an example to all of our local gentry?

Please do not think, dear listeners, that I am proposing him as an exemplar only in the matter of hunting. Not at all. Hunting was among the least of his talents. Besides that, he possessed a thousand other natural gifts both suitable and necessary to us of the gentry. He showed us how a true gentleman should go about consuming in one week everything produced in a year by the two thousand common people under his authority. He provided us with notable examples of how those two thousand people could, with good advantage, be whipped two or three times a year. He had a talent for dining sumptuously and elegantly on his estate when, presumably, Lent was being observed there. And this art produced some pleasant surprises for his guests. Yes, gentlemen, all this is true! It frequently happened that when we came to dine with him at his estate, and saw all of his peasants pallid and starving, we would be afraid that we ourselves would starve at his table. Looking at them, we would conclude that for a hundred versts around there was not a crust of bread or a consumptive chicken to be had. But what a pleasant surprise when we sat down at his table! On it was a wealth of victuals that one would have thought never existed in those parts – an abundance of which there was not the slightest hint elsewhere on his estates. Even the cleverest of us did not understand what he could still squeeze out of his peasants; and we were compelled to conclude that he had created his splendid banquets out of nothing.

But I see my enthusiasm is leading me astray from the order of thoughts I had intended to follow. Let us therefore consider the beginning of our hero's life. In this way we shall not miss one trait of those praiseworthy deeds of his – deeds that many of you, dear friends, are imitating most successfully. Let us, then, begin with his origins.

However much the philosophers may rave, claiming that in accordance with the genealogical table of the whole world we are all brothers, however often they may affirm that we are all the children of Adam, a person of gentle birth should be ashamed to own any such philosophy. And though it may be necessary and convenient that our servants should have descended from Adam, we would rather acknowledge that our original progenitor was an ass than to have the same origins as they. Nothing exalts a person so much as noble extraction: it is his chief merit. Let the philosophers protest that a grandee and a beggar are alike in body, soul, passions, foibles and virtues. If this be true, it is not the fault of the nobles. It is Nature's fault that she created them in the same form as the most vulgar commoners, so that we gentlemen have no special features to distinguish us. It is a sign of her laziness and negligence. I say no more than the truth, gentlemen! And if this Nature were a living being, she would be very ashamed of the fact that whereas she confers upon the lowliest worm those traits proper to his condition; whereas the smallest insect receives from her its colouring and capacities; whereas, when we consider the animal kingdom in its entirety, it seems to us that she is inexhaustible in her invention and variety – she, to her shame and our misfortune, has not invented anything at all by which to distinguish us from the peasants; has not so much as given us an extra finger as a sign of our superiority over the muzhiks. Does she not show greater concern for the butterflies than for the gentry? And so we must wear a sword – a thing, so it would seem, that we should have been born with. But in any case, thanks to our cleverness we have found ways of correcting her defects; and we have rid ourselves of the danger of being taken for animals of the same breed as the peasants.

Having a forefather who was wise, virtuous and useful to society – that is what makes a gentleman; that is what distinguishes him from the rabble and the common people, whose forefathers were neither wise, nor virtuous, nor useful to society. The more ancient and further removed from us our ancestors are, the more illustrious our noble strain. And it is precisely that which distinguishes our hero, of whom I make bold to invent fitting oblation; for it has been more than three hundred years since a wise and virtuous man appeared in his family. And that one man performed so many shining deeds that among his descendants no more such things were necessary; so that right up to the present they have been quite content to do without wise and virtuous men, and have lost none of their merit in the process.

Finally our hero, Jinglehead, made his appearance. He did not yet know what he was; but already his noble soul sensed the advantages of his birth, and in his second year he began to scratch the eyes of his wet nurse, and bite her ears. "That child will go far!" his father exclaimed rapturously, on one such occasion. "He doesn't yet know how to give orders, but he is already learning how to administer punishment. It is easy to see that he has noble blood in his veins." And the old man often wept for joy when he saw with what a noble demeanour his offspring pinched the wet nurse or the domestics. Not a single day passed but what our little hero scratched somebody. And as early as his fifth year he became aware that he was surrounded with the kind of hoi polloi that he could bite and scratch whenever he felt like it.

His all-knowing father was quick to realize that his son now needed a companion. There were a good many impoverished gentry living in that part of the country, but he was unwilling to stoop so low as to allow his son to share his time with such people. As for providing him with a serf's son as a companion, that struck the old gentleman as even more intolerable. Another person would not have known what to do. But the father of our hero immediately relieved this distressing situation: he gave his son, as a companion, a handsome spaniel. This, perhaps, is the underlying reason why our hero, for all of his life, preferred dogs to people and enjoyed himself more with the former than the latter.

Jinglehead, being accustomed to giving orders, received his new companion rather roughly, and started things off by pulling her ears. But little Pepper (for such was the dog's name) showed him that it is sometimes a mistake to play jokes on others, relying too much on one's own strength: she bit his arm till it bled. Our hero froze in astonishment. It was the first time he had encountered such a harsh response to his habitual behaviour. Never before had he been punished for his pinching. His heart was seething within him. But at the same time, he was afraid to have a taste of combat with Pepper. And so he ran to his father to complain of the mortal insult he had received from his new companion. "My boy," his incomparable father said to him, "don't you have plenty of serfs around you to pinch? Why did you have to bother Pepper? After all, a dog is not a servant: you have to be more careful with a dog, unless you want to get bitten. She is stupid. She can't be kept quiet and made to endure hardships without opening her mouth, like an intelligent being."

The precept deeply touched the heart of our young hero, and he never forgot it. As he grew up, he often engaged in those profound reflections for which this precept had provided the basis. He sought to discover ways of beating his domestic animals without exposing himself to danger, and of making them as passive as his peasants. Or at any rate he sought to discover why the former were impertinent enough to snap back more than the latter did; and he concluded that his peasants were inferior to his domestic animals.

His doting father, having noticed that the child was beginning to think, decided that the time had come to begin his education; and he himself undertook to teach him his ABCs. In five months the pupil had surpassed his teacher and was spelling in modern Russian at least as well as his father could. Such progress frightened the old man. He was afraid that his son might learn to read fluently, and that he might take it into his head, some day, to become an academician. And so the lad's course in philology ended with the last page of the ABC book. "That's enough reading and writing for you," his father said. "You should be ashamed of learning anything more. I want you to be a distinguished gentleman. It wouldn't be fitting for you to read books."

Our hero profited from this brilliant reasoning, and learnt to love all books like the plague. Not a single one found access to him, except for Rousseau's pronouncements on the harmfulness of knowledge. That was one work that earned his approbation, because of its epigraph. True, he never read that one either; but he always kept it on the mantelpiece. "Just read that," he would say, when anyone chanced to praise knowledge in his presence. "Read that, and you will regret being more intelligent than my bay horse. Oh, what a great man Rousseau was!"

94

he would continue. And afterwards he would undertake, slavishly, to count the pages in the book. This was his greatest concession to scholarship, and one that he made only to the author of *La Nouvelle Héloïse*.

Finally it came time for him to enter the civil service; and his rare progenitor, when bidding farewell to his son, delivered his last instructions to him. "Always remember, my darling son," he said, "that you are the owner of two thousand serfs. Remember that you are a gentleman of ancient stock, and the last of your line. Therefore, be sparing of yourself and don't follow the example of those unfortunates who, not having a crust of bread to eat, are obliged to wear out their health in the service. Behave in such a way as to avoid dismissal, and don't worry about the rest. Let the poor people seek promotions if they want to. As for us men of wealth, it is the promotions that should seek us out. Be always decorous in your behaviour; that is, don't venture outside the antechambers of important personages. Above all, avoid incurring the displeasure of a woman, of whatever low condition she may appear to be. The outward show of a woman's social station is like a young sapling: however weak and wretched it may seem, it often has roots that, deep down in the earth, are intertwined with those of a mighty oak which may crush you with its weight. In short, here is my testament in a nutshell: I want you to retire with high rank, not high honours." Whereupon he gave him his parental blessing and two thousand roubles for the journey. Three days after his son's departure, his illustrious life came to an end.

For all the eagerness of our hero to profit from these instructions, his noble soul accepted them only reluctantly.

Or to put it more precisely, he approved but half of them. That is, in accordance with his father's advice, he did not want to work; yet on the other hand he did not want to grow old sitting in antechambers. These two principles estranged him from two of his uncles, and from the government service, and made of him a philosopher. The frivolities of high society soon became tiresome to him. He noticed that wherever he went, either he himself yawned, or others yawned at him. And so he conceived the peaceable intention of withdrawing from the world, having everywhere seen indications that he and it were not suited to each other.

A rare magnanimity and an incomparable modesty – these two amiable qualities were manifest in him from the time he first arrived in the capital. In his place, and possessed of his illustrious family connections, a vulgarly ambitious man would not have remained aloof from high society. Rather, he would have sought entry into the best homes. But not our hero: he sat all night long in the taverns. He fled the life of elegance, and often, after passing the evening with a gang of zealous gamblers, he would return modestly home minus his coat. He never held a grudge, and he would go to dine, quite undisturbed, in the same place where, at supper the night before, he had taken a thrashing. He was forbearing to the extreme. I myself have witnessed, gentlemen, with what touching meekness he would take blows from his friends, and then drown his sorrows in drinking with them.

I repeat: an ambitious man, in his place, would have been seduced by the worldly vanities and examples of high society. But not he. When he heard that someone of his own age had received a decoration, that another person had been given an appointment, and another an award, he remained indifferent. None of these things touched his great soul, and he would listen to such news with a yawn. "It may very well be," he would say, "that some day I shall have to feed half of these civil servants. It's enough that I have two thousand serfs: that kind of rank will always assure me first place in my part of the country." Usually he concluded his comments with the words: "Vanity of vanities". And then, surrounding himself with a dozen bottles of port, he would sit down to a game of faro.

From this you can easily deduce, gentlemen, that the company he kept, while not elegant, was sportive. True, civil servants sometimes mingled with them; but as a rule the first two dozen bottles would establish complete equality and friendship in the gathering. However, this was not a tiresome kind of friendship, carried on for five years or so. No, it was a free and noble camaraderie, such that frequently, even before they had concluded their mutual pledges of affection, they would be pulling at each other's hair – quite without malice, of course, and often merely to pass the time.

There, gentlemen, you have a picture of his life in the city. He did not go in pursuit of happiness, but sought pleasures of another kind. He did not make the rounds, paying social calls at great houses, only to yawn with boredom. Instead, being a lover of freedom, he would often go to sleep under the table at his own friendly gatherings. He had no aspirations towards attracting, some day, the attention of the whole world upon himself: it was enough for him that his name was well known in all the taverns and coffee houses. And he had no intention of ever becoming a statesman. Not that he was lacking in intelligence; on the contrary, gentlemen, he was only too clever. It often happened that for this very reason he was given a thrashing by his companions of the card table, where he chiefly made a show of sharp wits. But since intelligence is persecuted everywhere in the world, he very soon tired of being intelligent and began to play cards with philosophical naivety and a noble trust in the honesty of others. His friends, instead of being impressed by these amiable traits, cleaned him out of his entire fortune in two months' time and left our philosopher half-naked – despite the fact that the northern climate is ill-suited to the practice of ascetic philosophy.

Anyone else, under such distressing circumstances, would have lost heart. Anyone else would have become desperate. But not he. Without the slightest vacillation he simply stayed at home, waiting with great and heartfelt humility for his creditors to take him off to jail. Like Julius Caesar, he did not try to escape his fate. He did not even go beyond his front gate, although in the darkness of the night he could have walked along the street in only his sleeveless jacket and slippers without violating the decorum of the city. Nor did he seek any help in his misfortune. "What must be, must be," he said, and yawned fearlessly.

And destiny rewarded him for his faith. Just at the moment when it seemed that he had been abandoned by the whole world; when all doors were closed to him except the doors of the city jail; when in his kitchen, as in Rome, there remained not a trace of its former glory; and – most catastrophic of all – when his famished cat, looking for a stale crust of bread with all the zeal of Columbus seeking the New World, knocked over and broke his last bottle of port – when, I say, all these misfortunes had been heaped upon him, one of his uncles, renowned for his parsimony, in the practice of which he had gone without supper for twenty years, finally decided not to eat dinner either, and so left our hero an inheritance of five thousand serfs and 100,000 roubles.

Do you suppose this turned him into a proud man? Not a bit of it! That very same evening he went to see a wine merchant of his acquaintance, had a drinking bout with him, and then very modestly spent the night at his establishment, lying on a bare brick floor.

But already his passions were on the wane. And so, profiting from his past misfortunes, he no longer desired to seek good luck in any suit of cards whatsoever. He obtained a rank in the civil service and then retired, having decided to return to his country estate in order to embellish our district with his presence. Since he had a pronounced dislike for noisy farewell ceremonies, he left the city without notifying a single creditor. Then too, it may have been because of his modesty that he favoured the French custom of leaving without saying goodbye, since the most reliable billiard-scorers have testified that, whenever he could, he took French leave of the taverns, however strongly they reproached him for it.

And so at last he withdrew from the bustle of the city and entered into a new field for the testing of his talents. And you, my friends, have seen for yourselves how brightly those talents shone.

No sooner had he arrived here, than he declared open war against the hares and assembled a numerous army of hounds. Having the interests of the peasants at heart, he was resolved to exterminate the entire race of hares. And he kept his word. True, many of his perverse peasants

99

complained that they would rather feed the hares than an infinite number of hounds and a useless gang of hunters; that they would rather encounter hares in the grain fields than a few dozen horses and twice as many hounds. But our hero, who knew just when and where to whip such tellers of idle tales, quieted their grumblings and persisted in his implacable hatred of the hares, like that of Hannibal towards the Romans.

In order to be more certain of extirpating them, he felled and sold his timber, meanwhile reducing the peasants to such a state that they had nothing wherewith to sow the fields. Imagine, if you will, the inner satisfaction felt by our hero as he rode out to the fields and found them clean as a tablecloth, so that he was free of all apprehension that a hare could conceal itself anywhere whatsoever. In three years he had cleared his land so completely that the intrepid beasts could find nothing there but death from starvation. "Tell me," someone once asked him, "wouldn't you rather see a thousand well-fed hares on your land than five thousand hungry peasants? Isn't a man a fool if he burns down his house to get rid of the cockroaches?"

"Hold your tongue!" our hero replied. "I know very well that my peasants have nothing to eat. But in another five years the hares will abandon my land. They will flee from it as from a desert. And when that time comes, I will outwit that entire breed of cowardly plunderers by restoring the order and abundance of the past."

Ah, my friends, what a penetrating mind! Was there ever anyone, at any time, who conceived such a bold and majestic enterprise? Nero burnt the splendid city of Rome in order to extirpate a handful of Christians. Julius Caesar killed off great numbers of his fellow citizens

100

because he wanted to put down the power of Pompey, which was harmful to them. Alexander the Great cut his way through many kingdoms with the sword, conquering and destroying thousands of tribes, apparently so that he could wet his boots in the ocean surf and then brag about it back home. But none of these schemes or labours can compare with the feats of our hero. The others destroyed men in order to gain glory; but he destroyed them in order to stamp out hares.

And yet destiny, ever jealous of great deeds, did not allow him to consummate his scheme. In this he was like many other heroes who, having undertaken to perform a thousand feats in two years' time, have died in the first or second year of their enterprise.

Such, gentlemen, are the feats of our hero, which... But what's this? My amiable auditors have gently dozed off. Their venerable heads are at rest, like so many big, plump melons, around the punchbowl. O my dear departed friend, glory in thy triumph! Thy friends, who love thee, have inherited thy ways! For it was precisely thus that thou wert wont to doze off, at those jolly nocturnal revels, with thy nose half-submerged in a bowl of ale. If thou canst, absent thee from grim Pluto for a while, and look up from beneath the floor at thy friends. Then triumphantly tell the other dwellers in the infernal regions what a pleasant effect was produced by this panegyric in thy honour. And a fig for the disapproving stare of those envious authors who believe that they alone have obtained from Apollo the privilege of putting this world to sleep with their works!

A Tale of How One Muzhik Looked after Two Generals*

Mikhail Saltykov

O NCE UPON A TIME there were two generals. They were both nitwits, and so in no time at all, by a wave of some magic wand, they found themselves on a desert island.

The two generals had spent all their lives in some kind of registry office: there they had been born and brought up, and there they had grown old. Consequently, they didn't understand anything at all. They didn't even understand any words except: "With assurance of the highest esteem, I remain, Your Most Humble Servant…"

The registry office had been abolished as superfluous, and the two generals had been let go. They had settled down to retirement in Petersburg, on Podyacheskaya Street, in separate apartments. Each of them had a woman to cook for him, and each collected a pension. But then suddenly they found themselves on a desert island. They woke up and lo! They were both lying under the same blanket. Of course, at first they didn't grasp the situation and began to talk to one another as though nothing had happened.

"I had a strange dream just now, Your Excellency," said one of the generals. "It was just as if I was living on a desert island."

Having uttered these words, up he jumped. So did the other general.

"Good Heavens! What's going on here?" they both cried out in amazement.

And they began pinching each other to find out whether this strange thing had happened to them in reality, or only in a dream. But no matter how hard they tried to convince themselves that it was all nothing more than a dream, they had to acknowledge the sad reality.

Before them, the sea stretched away to one side; on the other side lay a small clump of earth beyond which the same boundless sea stretched away again. The generals wept for the first time since the registry office had been closed.

They began looking each other over, and noticed that they were in their nightshirts, and that each had an order* hung around his neck.

"I'd certainly give a lot for a cup of coffee right now!" said one of the generals. But then he recalled what an outlandish thing had happened, and began to weep again. "What are we going to do?" he continued through his tears. "If we wrote a report right now, what earthly good would it do?"

"I'll tell you what, Your Excellency," the other general said. "You go east, and I'll go west, and towards evening we'll both come back here. Who knows? Perhaps we'll find something."

They started trying to find out which direction was east and which was west. They remembered that their departmental chief had once said: "If you want to find the east, stand so that you're facing north, and the east will be on your right." So they started trying to find which was north. They faced this way and that, they tried every point of the compass; but since they had spent all their lives in the registry office, they didn't find anything.

"I'll tell you what, Your Excellency. You go to the right and I'll go to the left – that's the best." This was said by the general who, in addition to his service at the registry office, had been a penmanship teacher at a school for soldiers' sons, and was consequently a bit less stupid than the other.

No sooner said than done. One of the generals set off to the right, and came upon some trees with all kinds of fruit on them. He wanted to pick at least one apple, but they were all so high above the ground that he would have to climb the tree. He tried to climb it, but without success: all he managed to do was tear his nightshirt.

Next he came to a brook, and saw it was teeming with fish – just like the fish farm on the Fontanka.*

"How fine it would be to have fish like that and be back home on Podyacheskaya Street!" he thought, his mouth watering so much that it changed the very expression on his face.

He went on into the woods: the hazel grouse were whistling, the black grouse were drumming, and the hares were scampering about.

"Good Lord, just think of all that food!" he said, so hungry by now he was starting to feel sick to his stomach.

But there wasn't a thing he could do about it, and he had to return empty-handed to the rendezvous point. When he got there the other general was waiting for him.

"Well, how did it go, Your Excellency? Did you get anything?"

"Just this old copy of the *Moscow News** that I came across. Nothing more."

The generals again lay down to sleep, but they were too hungry. First they would fret over who might be getting their pensions; then they would remember the fruit, fish, grouse and hares they had seen that day.

"Who would have thought, Your Excellency, that human food, in its original form, flies, swims and grows on trees?" said one of the generals.

"Yes," answered the other, "I must confess that until now I always thought that breakfast rolls came into the world in the very same shape in which they are served with the morning coffee."

"Hence it follows that if, for example, a person wants to eat a partridge, he must first catch it, kill it, pluck it and roast it... But how does one do all that?"

"But how does one do all that?" the other general repeated, just like an echo.

They lapsed into silence and tried to fall asleep; but hunger had driven off sleep for good. Grouse, turkeys and suckling pigs kept flashing before their mind's eye, succulent, done to a turn, garnished with pickles, relish and other fixings.

"Right now I think I could eat one of my own boots!" said one general.

"Gloves can be tasty too," sighed the other general, "when they've been worn a long time."

Suddenly the two generals looked at each other: there was an evil gleam in their eyes, their teeth were snapping, and a low growl issued from their chests. They began slowly to creep towards each other, and the next instant both were raging with bloodlust. Handfuls of hair and rent clothing swirled about in the air, which resounded with squeals and groans. The general who had been a

108

teacher of penmanship bit off his colleague's decoration and gobbled it up. But the sight of blood seemed to bring them back to their senses.

"God help us!" they both cried out at once. "Why, at this rate we'll be eating each other!"

"But how do we happen to be here? Who was the villain that played such a trick on us?"

"The thing to do, Your Excellency," said one of the generals, "is to keep our minds occupied with some kind of conversation. Otherwise, murder will be done here."

"Commence!" said the other.

"Well, just for example. Why is it, do you think, that the sun first rises and then sets, instead of the other way around?"

"You're a droll fellow, Your Excellency! Don't you yourself first rise, then go to the office and do your paperwork, and then lie down to sleep?"

"But why not a different arrangement of things? Why don't I lie down first, have various kinds of dreams, and *then* rise?"

"Hm... yes, I suppose... And yet I must confess, when I was still working at my office I always thought of it like this: 'Now it's morning, next will come the day, then they'll serve dinner, and then it will be time to go to bed.'"

But the mention of dinner threw them both into despondency and nipped that little conversation in the bud. "I was told by a doctor I know that a man can nourish himself on his own juices for a long time," one of the generals resumed.

"But how?"

"It's simple. It seems that your own juices produce other juices, and these in turn produce still other juices, until finally you run out of juices."

"And then what?"

"Then you have to eat something."

"Oh, damnation!"

In short, no matter what the generals started to talk about, it always ended up by reminding them of food, and this whetted their appetites even more. They decided to break off the conversation and, remembering the copy of the *Moscow News* they had found, they began avidly to read it.

In a voice vibrant with emotion, one of them read:

"Yesterday the venerable mayor of our ancient capital gave a banquet. The table was set with dazzling splendour for a hundred persons. The tributes of all lands had made and kept, as it were, a rendezvous at this marvellous gala. They included "the golden sterlet from Sheksna",* the pheasant bred in the forests of the Caucasus, and strawberries – which are so rare in our northern clime in the month of February—"

"Damn it all, anyway!" the other general exclaimed in despair. "Can't you find something else to read about?" And snatching the paper from his colleague, he read the following:

"From our correspondent in Tula. Yesterday, on the occasion of the catching of a sturgeon in the Upa River (an event unprecedented in the memory of the

oldest local inhabitants, and all the more so since the sturgeon bore a distinct resemblance to the district police inspector), a banquet was held at the local club. The hero of the festivities was brought in on a huge wooden platter, garnished with gherkins and holding in its mouth a piece of membrane.* Dr P***, who acted as master of ceremonies on this occasion, took care to see that each of the guests got a morsel. The sauces were most varied and, one might even say, fanciful—"

"Pardon me, Your Excellency," the first general cut in, "but it seems that you yourself are not very prudent in your choice of reading matter." And seizing the paper in his turn, he began to read:

"From our correspondent in Vyatka. One of the oldest of the local inhabitants has devised the following original recipe for making fish soup. Take a live burbot, and first of all give it a lashing. Then when, as a result of its sorrows, its liver has become enlarged..."

The generals' heads drooped. Whatever their eyes fell upon reminded them of food. Even their own thoughts contrived mischief against them; for no matter how hard they tried to keep thoughts of steak from their minds, those thoughts forced their way in.

But suddenly the general who had been a teacher of penmanship was struck by an inspiration. "How about it, Your Excellency?" he said joyously. "Let's find ourselves a muzhik!"

"What do you mean 'a muzhik'?"

111

"Why, just an ordinary muzhik – one of the usual kind. He could serve us rolls right away, and catch grouse and fish for us."

"Hm... A muzhik... But where are we going to find this muzhik when there's no muzhik here?"

"What do you mean, 'no muzhik'? There's always a muzhik – everywhere! You just have to look for him. Most likely he's hiding somewhere so he won't have to work."

This idea heartened the generals so much that they jumped up in fine fettle and went off looking for a muzhik.

They wandered around the island for a long time without having any success. But at last the pungent odour of bran bread and sour-smelling sheepskin put them on the right track. Lying under a tree, belly up, with his hands under his head, a colossal muzhik was sleeping – avoiding work in the most brazen manner. The indignation of the two generals knew no bounds.

"So you're sleeping, lazybones!" they fumed at him. "Probably you don't care at all that there are two generals right in front of you who have been starving for two days. Hop to work this instant!"

The muzhik got up. He saw that the two generals were stern. He would have liked to show them a clean pair of heels, but they grabbed him and held on for dear life.

And so, with them watching him, he got to work. First thing, he climbed a tree and picked ten of the ripest apples for each of the generals. For himself he picked only one, and it was green. Next he dug around in the ground and got some potatoes. After that, he took two sticks of wood, rubbed them together, and made a fire. Then, using some of his own hair, he made a snare and caught a hazel grouse. Finally, he kindled the fire into a hot blaze, and over it he cooked so much food of all kinds that the generals even began to wonder whether they shouldn't give a little of it to this loafer.

The generals observed the muzhik's exertions, and their hearts leapt for joy. They had already forgotten that they had almost starved to death the day before. Instead, they thought: "What a splendid thing it is to be a general! Wherever you are, you're secure!"

Meanwhile, the huge muzhik kept asking them, "Will that do, masters?"

"Oh, yes, dear friend. We can see you're industrious," the generals replied.

"Then is it all right if I rest a little?"

"By all means, dear friend. But first make up a rope."

The huge muzhik promptly gathered some wild hemp, soaked it in water, pounded and dressed it; and by evening the rope was ready. With this rope the generals tied the big muzhik to a tree so he could not run away, and then they lay down to sleep.

One day went by, and then another, and the huge muzhik proved so clever that he even cooked soup in his cupped hands. The generals were happy, plump, well fed, and pampered-looking. They began telling each other that it wasn't costing them anything to live here, and meanwhile their pensions were piling up higher and higher.

"What do you think, Your Excellency?" one general would say to the other after breakfast. "Was there ever really a Tower of Babel? Or is it just some kind of allegory?"

"I think, Your Excellency, that it really happened. Otherwise how explain the existence of different languages on earth?"

"And so the Flood really happened too?"

"Yes, it really happened too. Otherwise, how explain the existence of antediluvian animals? Besides, the *Moscow News* says—"

"How about reading the *Moscow News* now?"

So they would find the copy of the newspaper, sit down in the shade, and read it from the front page to the last: about how people were eating in Moscow, eating in Tula, eating in Penza, eating in Ryazan. And everything was fine – they didn't even feel queasy.

But after a while – maybe a short one, maybe a long one* – the generals got bored. More and more often they would remember the cooks they had left behind in Petersburg; and they even shed a few tears on the sly.

"What do you suppose is happening now on Podyacheskaya Street, Your Excellency?" one general would ask the other.

"Oh, don't even talk about it, Your Excellency!" the other would reply. "My heart is so heavy with homesickness!"

"No two ways about it: the living is really good here. But still, you know, the young ram misses his yearling ewe, as they say. And one misses one's uniform too."

"I should say so! Especially if it's an actual state councillor's uniform.* Why, the gold braid alone is enough to dazzle you!"

And so they began nagging at the muzhik to get them back to Podyacheskaya Street. And what do you think? It turned out that the muzhik actually knew his way around Podyacheskaya Street. He had "been there, and drunk mead and beer, but it had run down his beard and never got into his mouth".*

"Why, we're Podyacheskaya Street generals!" they exclaimed joyously.

"And me?" replied the muzhik. "Maybe once you happened to see a man on scaffolding hung by a rope on the outside of a building, slapping paint on the wall, or crawling along the rooftop like a fly. If you did, that was me!"

And the muzhik began to ponder how to pleasure his two generals because they had been so kind to a loafer like him and had not scorned his lowly labours. So he built a ship – well, not really a ship but a vessel of sorts that would take you across the ocean sea and clear to Podyacheskaya Street.

"Just be careful you don't drown us, you scum!" said the generals, when they saw the boat bobbing on the waves.

"Don't worry, masters – this ain't the first time for me," the muzhik replied, and began making ready for their departure.

He gathered some swansdown of the softest kind and lined the boat's bottom with it. This done, he had the generals lie down in the bottom and, crossing himself, he shoved off.

How great was the generals' fright at the storms and various gales during that voyage, and how they berated that big muzhik for his laziness – this was something no man could write with a pen or tell in a tale.* But the muzhik just kept on rowing and rowing, and feeding the generals herring.

Then at last they sighted old Mother Neva, then the glorious canal named for Catherine, and finally Great Podyacheskaya Street.

When the cooks saw how well fed their generals were, how pampered-looking, and how happy, they threw up their hands in amazement. The generals drank their fill of coffee, stuffed themselves on sweet rolls, and put on their uniforms. Then they went to the Treasury; and the money they raked in there is something no man could write with a pen or tell in a tale.

Nor did they forget the muzhik. They sent him a small glass of vodka and a five-copeck piece.

Make merry, muzhik!

1869

The Eagle as Patron of the Arts*

Mikhail Saltykov

P OETS HAVE WRITTEN MANY verses about eagles, always in
their praise: the eagle's features are beautiful beyond
description; his glance is swift, and his flight majestic. He
does not fly, like other birds: he either soars or "spread-
eagles". Moreover, he stares straight at the sun, and he
contends with the thunderclaps. Some poets even endow
him with a magnanimous heart. If, for example, they
want to sing the praises of a policeman, they invariably
compare him to an eagle. They say, "Like an eagle, the
officer wearing badge number such-and-such located the
suspect, seized him, and, having heard his statement,
pardoned him."

For a long time, I myself believed these panegyrics. I
used to think: "Why, now, that's really fine! 'He seized
him... and pardoned him'!" *Pardoned* him! That's what I
found especially fascinating. Whom did the eagle pardon?
A mouse. And what is a mouse? So I'd run off hurry-
scurry to one of my poet friends and tell him about this
latest act of magnanimity on the part of the eagle. And
my poet friend would strike a pose, breathe deeply for a
moment, and then start belching out verses.

But one day it occurred to me: "Just why did the eagle
'pardon' the mouse? The mouse was scampering across
the road on his own business when the eagle saw him,
swooped down, crushed him into a bloody lump, and...
pardoned him! Why did *he* pardon the mouse, and not
vice versa?

119

The more I thought about it, the more doubts I had. I began to keep my eyes peeled and my ears perked up. Plainly, something was wrong. In the first place, an eagle certainly doesn't catch mice just in order to pardon them. In the second place, even supposing that the eagle did "pardon" the mouse, it really would have been much better if he had just left him alone. And finally, in the third place, even though he's an eagle – or, for that matter, an arch-eagle – he's still a bird. He is in fact so much a bird that only through a gross misunderstanding could a comparison to him be found flattering – even by a policeman.

And today my ideas on eagles are as follows: eagles are eagles, and that's all they are. They are predatory and carnivorous; but it can be said by way of justification that nature herself fitted them out to be antivegetarians. And since they are, at one and the same time, powerful, long-sighted, swift and merciless, it is only natural that at the sight of them all other denizens of the air make haste to hide. But this is owing to fright, and not to rapture – as some of the poets would have it. Also, eagles always live in isolation, in inaccessible places. They do not spend their time dispensing hospitality but in plundering; and when they are not plundering, they doze.

There was once, however, an eagle who got bored with living in isolation, so he said to his eagless, "This is a damned dull life – just the two of us, always together! And you can get feeble-minded from staring at the sun all day."

So he began to ponder. And the more he pondered, the more it seemed to him that it would be good to lead the kind of life the landowners did in the old days. He would assemble a household of menials and live like a king.

The crows would report all the nasty gossip; the parrots would turn somersaults for him; the magpie would cook his porridge; starlings would sing paeans in praise of him; the common owls, owlets and eagle owls would fly night patrols; and the hawks, vultures and falcons would catch game for him. And he himself would have nothing else to do but be bloodthirsty.

He thought and thought, and finally made up his mind. So one day he summoned a hawk, a vulture and a falcon, and said to them: "Assemble for me a household of menials such as the landowners had in the old days. They will provide amusement for me, and I will tyrannize over them. That is all."

Having received their orders, these birds of prey flew off in different directions. They got things off to a fast start, with no playing around. First of all, they drove in a whole horde of crows. They herded them in, registered them in the census lists, and gave them tax forms. Now, crows are fertile birds, and docile. But the best thing about them is that they so well represent the "muzhik" class of society. And everybody knows that if the "dear little muzhiks" are on hand, the job is as good as done – except for a few details that are easily managed. And the latter were managed. The corncrakes and loons were organized into a brass band; the parrots were dressed up as buffoons; the magpie, seeing that he was a thief, was given the keys to the Treasury; and the owlets and eagle owls were assigned to fly night patrol. In short, they set up an establishment that no nobleman would have been ashamed of. They didn't even forget the cuckoo: they appointed him soothsayer to the eagless, and built a foundling home for cuckoo orphans.

But scarcely had they put the regulations of the establishment into effect, when they realized that something was lacking. For a long time they puzzled their heads over what it was, and finally they hit on it. In every nobleman's establishment the arts and sciences should be represented; but the eagle's had neither.

Three birds in particular considered this oversight personally offensive: the bullfinch, the woodpecker and the nightingale. The bullfinch was a clever fellow, and had been whistling since adolescence. He had got his primary education at a school for soldiers' sons, and then become a regimental clerk. Once having learnt how to use punctuation marks, he began to publish – without prior censorship – a newspaper called the *Forest Herald*. But he just couldn't make a go of things. Whatever subject he brought up was one he shouldn't have. Whatever he *didn't* bring up was something he not only could have but should have. And for this he kept getting his ears boxed. So he decided: "I'll join the eagle's establishment. What do I care if he orders me to proclaim his fame every morning, so long as I don't get hurt?"

The woodpecker was a modest scholar, and led a strictly solitary life. He never associated with anyone at all. (He was even thought by many to be a hard drinker, like all serious scholars.) Instead, he would sit for whole days on the branch of a pine tree, pecking away. And he pecked out a whole batch of historical articles: 'The Genealogy of the Wood Sprite'; 'Was Baba-Yaga* Married?'; 'Under Which Sex Should Witches Be Registered in the Census Lists?', and so on. But, peck as he would, he couldn't find a publisher for his pamphlets. And so he decided: "I'll enter the eagle's service as one of his court historians. Maybe he'll have my articles published at the crows' expense!"

As for the nightingale, he couldn't complain about how life had treated him. From time immemorial, he had sung so sweetly that not only the tall, straight pines but even the merchants in the Moscow bazaar had been stirred upon hearing him. All the world loved him, and all the world held its breath and listened as, perched in some thicket, he poured forth his sweet songs. But he was sensual and vain beyond all measure. It was not enough that he made the woods resound with his untrammelled song. It was not enough that he drenched grieving hearts in his music. He kept thinking of how the eagle would hang a necklace of ant eggs around his neck, or decorate his whole breast with live cockroaches;* and of how the eagless would arrange secret trysts with him in the moonlight. To make a long story short, the three birds kept pestering the falcon to plead their cause to the eagle.

The eagle listened closely – right through to the end – to the falcon's report on the necessity of introducing the arts and sciences, but he didn't understand it right away. He just sat there clacking his beak and flexing his talons; and his eyes glittered in the sunlight like polished gems. He had never so much as seen a newspaper; he had no interest in Baba-Yaga or other witches; and as for the nightingale, he had heard only one thing about it: that it was a small bird, and not worth soiling one's beak on.

"I dare say you don't know that Bonaparte is dead?" asked the falcon.

"Who is this Bonaparte?"

"See what I mean? And that's something worth knowing too. Some of these days you'll be having guests, and

123

they'll start up a conversation. They'll say, 'That was in Bonaparte's time,' and you'll just look blank. That's not good."

The common owl was called in for advice, and he reaffirmed that the arts and sciences should be introduced into the establishment, since life would then be made interesting for the eagles. And besides, said he, there was nothing shameful about taking an objective view of things. "Knowledge is light, but ignorance is darkness. Anybody can eat and sleep. But just try to solve the problem that begins 'A flock of geese were flying...' and you're in trouble. In the old days the clever landowners always figured one man who could read and write was worth two illiterates. In other words, they realized that education was useful. Just take the siskin, for example. All his education consists in knowing how to carry a pail of water. But what money they pay for that! I can see in the dark, and for this they have called me wise. You stare at the sun for hours on end without blinking, and what they say about you is: 'The eagle is skilful, but he's a nitwit.'"

"Well, I'm not downright *against* education!" clacked the eagle.

No sooner said than done. The next day a "Golden Age" began in the eagle's establishment. The starlings memorized the anthem, 'Education Nourishes Youth'. The corncrakes and loons practised on the trumpet; the parrots worked up some new stunts. Another tax was levied on the crows, under the name of "educational tax"; a cadet corps was founded for the young falcons and young hawks; an Académie des Sciences was established for the common owls, the eagle owls, and the owlets; and a penny primer was purchased for each of the young crows.

Finally, the oldest starling was made poet laureate under the name of Vasily Kirilych Tredyakovsky,* and instructed to make ready for a contest with the nightingale on the following day.

The eagerly awaited day arrived. The new recruits were brought before the eagle and ordered to display their talents.

The bullfinch was most successful. Instead of making a speech of welcome, he read a humorous sketch from a newspaper – one so frothy that even the eagle thought he understood it. The bullfinch said that the best thing to do was live high on the hog; and the eagle approved with, "That's right!" He said that his retail sales were good, and he didn't care about anything else; and the eagle approved with, "That's right!" He said that the servant had a better life than the master, because the master has many worries but the servant doesn't have to worry about the master; and the eagle approved: "That's right!" He said that back when he still had a conscience he went around with no trousers, but now that he hadn't one iota of conscience left, he wore two pairs of trousers at once; and the eagle approved: "That's right!"

Finally the bullfinch became a bore. "Next!" clacked the eagle.

The woodpecker began by saying that the genealogy of the eagle went back to the Sun; and the eagle confirmed this on his own part, saying, "I heard something like that from my dad."

"The Sun," said the woodpecker, "had three children: a daughter, the Shark; and two sons, the Lion and the Eagle. The Shark was a harlot; and for this her father imprisoned her in the depths of the ocean. The Lion forsook his father; so the Sun made him sovereign of the wastelands. But the Eagle was a respectful son, so the father established him closer to himself, making him ruler over the realms of the air."

But the woodpecker had hardly pecked his way through the introduction to his learned paper, when the eagle screamed impatiently, "Next! Next!"

Then the nightingale began to sing, and right away he got into trouble. He sang of the joy of the servant upon learning that God has sent him a landowner for a master; he sang of the generosity of the eagles who don't begrudge their servants an occasional tip. But no matter how hard he tried to sound fashionably servile, he couldn't make it fit in with his innate "artistry". He himself was every inch a flunkey (he had even come up with a second-hand white cravat from somewhere, and had his hair tightly curled), but his "art" couldn't be kept within the bounds of servility: it kept bursting out into the open. Sing as he might, the eagle didn't understand him; and that was that.

"What is that nincompoop mumbling about?" he yelled finally. "Call Tredyakovsky!"

Vasily Kirilych was there in a hop, a skip and a jump. He took up the same servile themes, but he spelt them out so plainly that the eagle kept repeating: "That's right! That's right! That's right!" When the contest was over the eagle hung a necklace of ant eggs around Tredyakovsky's neck and, his eyes flashing with wrath at the nightingale, he screamed, "Get that bum out of here!"

This put an end to the nightingale's ambitious efforts. Quickly, they bundled him off to the market and sold him to the Parting Friends Tavern, where to this day he pours his sweet poison into the hearts of those customers so soused that they are feeling "meteoric".

Nevertheless, the pursuit of enlightenment was not abandoned. The young hawks and falcons continued to attend school; the Académie des Sciences undertook to publish a dictionary and vanquished half of the letter "A"; and the woodpecker completed the tenth volume of his *History of Wood Sprites*. But the bullfinch lay low. From the very first day he had sensed that all this commotion about culture would come to a speedy and ungracious end; and apparently his premonitions were well founded.

The thing was that the common owl and the falcon, who had assumed the direction of these educational activities, had made a big mistake: they had conceived the idea of teaching the eagle himself to read and write. They used the phonetic method, which is easy and interesting; but for all their strenuous efforts, after a year the eagle was still signing his name "Easel" instead of "Eagle", with the result that no self-respecting creditor would accept a promissory note with that signature on it. But an even bigger mistake was this: following the general pattern of pedagogues, neither the owl nor the falcon gave the eagle any time off. The owl was constantly breathing down his neck and screeching, "A... B... C..." And the falcon, just as constantly, kept harping that if the eagle didn't learn the first four rules of arithmetic, he couldn't divide up the game plunder.

"Let's suppose you steal ten goslings. If you give two to the police clerk and eat one, how many are left?" the falcon would ask reproachfully.

The eagle could never figure it out, and so he kept still. But with each passing day he harboured more and more wrath in his heart against the falcon.

Relations became strained, and a group of intriguers were quick to take advantage of the situation. The vulture headed up the plot, and he soon got the cuckoo to join him. The latter started whispering to the eagless, "They're undoing our lord and master with all this teaching. They're torturing him."

And the eagless began to taunt the eagle, "Oh, you scholar! You professor, you!"

Then, by means of their joint efforts, they aroused "dark desires" in the hawk.

And one morning at daybreak, when the eagle had just woken up, the owl crept up on him from behind, as usual, and began buzzing: "R... S... T—"

"Go away, you pest!" the eagle growled – but rather gently.

"Your Eagleship, please be so kind as to repeat after me: U... V—"

"*Go away*, I said."

"W... X... Y—"

In one instant the eagle turned on the owl and ripped him in two.

An hour later, knowing nothing of what had happened, the falcon came back from his morning's hunting. "Here's a problem for you," he said. "Supposing the night's plunder comes to seventy-two pounds of game. If we divide it into two equal parts – one for you and one for all your menials – how much will you get as your share?"

"All of it," answered the eagle.

"Come, now – be serious," objected the falcon. "If the answer had been 'all of it', I wouldn't even have asked you the question."

It wasn't the first time the falcon had given him such a problem to solve; but this time the tone he adopted struck the eagle as intolerable. It made his blood boil to think that when he had said "all of it", his servant had dared to contradict him. Now, it is well known that an eagle, when his blood starts to boil, can't tell the difference between pedagogical methods and a treasonous plot. And this eagle acted accordingly.

However, after liquidating the falcon, he stipulated, "But the des Sciences Académie will remain as before."

Once again the starlings sang 'Education Nourishes Youth', but it was plain to everybody that the Golden Age was drawing to a close. Up ahead loomed the darkness of ignorance, with its inseparable companions: civil discord and strife of all kinds.

The strife began with the appearance of two claimants, the vulture and the hawk, for the position of the deceased falcon. And since both rivals concentrated their attention exclusively on their own interests, public affairs were relegated to second place and gradually fell into neglect. In a month's time, not a trace of the recent Golden Age remained. The starlings got lazy; the corncrakes began to play out of tune; the magpie stole left and right; and the crows got so far behind on their taxes that mass floggings had to be resorted to. Things even reached the point where the eagle and eagless were being served spoilt meat.

In order to clear themselves of any responsibility for this mess, the hawk and the vulture teamed up temporarily, and put all the blame on enlightenment. Education, said they, is no doubt useful, but only when times are right for it. Our grandfathers got along without education, and so can we.

By way of proving that all the harm came from education, they began discovering plots; and those plots always involved a book of some kind – if only a prayer book. Then came a spate of searches, investigations and trials...

"That's all!" rang out from on high. It was the eagle. Enlightenment had run its course.

Such a silence now reigned all through the establishment that one could even hear the slanderous whisperings as they crawled along the ground.

The first victim of the new climate of ideas was the woodpecker. God knows the poor little bird was innocent! But he knew how to read and write, and that was ample grounds for his indictment.

"Do you know how to use punctuation marks?"

"Yes, not only the usual ones but such rare ones as quotation marks, hyphens and parentheses. I always use them conscientiously."

"And can you tell the feminine gender from the masculine?"

"Yes, I can. I wouldn't confuse them even in the darkness of night."

That settled it. They put him in chains and imprisoned him in a hollow tree for life. And the next day he died there, having been eaten alive by ants.

This business of the woodpecker was scarcely over when it was followed by a pogrom in the Académie des Sciences. However, the owlets and eagle owls defended themselves stoutly; they didn't like the idea of giving up the well-heated apartments provided for them by the government. They said they weren't pursuing the sciences in order to popularize them but rather to protect them from the evil eye. But the vulture at once punctured this subterfuge by asking, "Why have science at all?" This question took them by surprise, and they couldn't answer it. So they were sold off separately to truck gardeners, who stuffed them as scarecrows and set them out to protect their vegetable gardens.

At the same time the penny primers were taken away from the young crows and mashed into a pulp from which playing cards were made.

The longer it went on, the worse it got. The owls were followed by the starlings, the corncrakes, the parrots, the siskins... Even the deaf black grouse was suspected of "having opinions" because he kept quiet all day and slept at night.

The establishment dwindled. There remained only the eagle and eagless, together with the hawk and the vulture, while in the distance was the horde of crows, who kept on multiplying quite shamelessly. And the more they multiplied, the higher their back taxes piled up.

Then the hawk and the vulture, not knowing whom else to destroy (the crows didn't count), set out to destroy each other, and all on the grounds of education. The hawk informed on the vulture, reporting that he was reading a prayer book in secret; and the vulture falsely accused the hawk of keeping a songbook concealed in a hollow tree.

The eagle was quite at a loss what to do.

But at that moment, History itself stepped up its flow in order to put an end to all this turmoil. Something most extraordinary occurred. The crows, noticing they had been left untended, suddenly wondered: "Let's see. What was it the penny primer said on this subject?" But before they could rightly remember, the whole flock instinctively took off and flew away.

The eagle started after them, but it was no go: the easy life in the style of the landowners had made him so flabby he could scarcely flap his wings.

Then he turned to his wife and said, "Let this be a lesson to all eagles!"

But just what the word "lesson" meant in this case – whether education was bad for eagles, or eagles were bad for education, or both at once – he didn't say.

1886

The Tale of Ivan the Fool

and His Two Brothers, Semyon the Soldier and Taras the Big-Belly, and of His Sister, Malanya the Deaf-Mute, and of the Old Devil and the Three Imps

Leo Tolstoy

1

I N A CERTAIN KINGDOM in a certain land there once lived a rich peasant. And the rich peasant had three sons – Semyon the Soldier, Taras the Big-Belly and Ivan the Fool – and one daughter, Malanya the Deaf-Mute. Semyon the Soldier went to war to serve the Tsar, Taras the Big-Belly went to a merchant's in the city to become a trader, and Ivan the Fool stayed at home with his sister to work in the fields.

Semyon the Soldier won high rank and an estate, and married a nobleman's daughter. His pay was big and his estate was big, but he still couldn't make ends meet. Whatever he took in, his high-born wife squandered it all, and they never had any money.

When Semyon went to his estate to collect the income, his steward said to him, "We don't have anything to earn money with. We don't have any horses, or milk cows, or other livestock, or tools, or a plough or harrow. We must get these first – then there'll be an income."

So Semyon the Soldier went to his father. "You are rich, Father," he said, "but you have never given me anything. Give me a third of what you have, and I'll add it to my estate."

But the old man said, "You never made any contribution when you were here at home. Why should I give you a third? It wouldn't be fair to Ivan and the girl."

Semyon said, "But after all, he's a fool and she's deaf and dumb. What good is it to them?"

Then the old man said, "It's up to Ivan."

And Ivan said, "Well, why not? Let him take it."

So Semyon the Soldier took the portion of his father's property and added it to his own estate, and then went off to serve the Tsar again.

Taras the Big-Belly also acquired a lot of money, and married a merchant's daughter. But his income still wasn't enough; so he came to his father and said, "Give me my share."

But the old man was not willing to give Taras his portion, either. "You never contributed anything when you were here at home. Everything in this house was brought in by Ivan. Besides, it wouldn't be fair to him and the girl."

But Taras said, "What good is it to him? He's a fool. He'll never get married, because nobody will have him. And a girl who's a deaf-mute doesn't need anything, either. Come on, Ivan," he said. "Give me half of the grain, and as for the livestock, all I want to take is the big grey stallion. You can't use him for ploughing, anyway."

Ivan laughed. "Well, why not?" he said. "I'll go and put a halter on him."

So they gave Taras his portion too. He hauled the grain into town, and led away the grey stallion. Ivan was left with one old grey mare to go on with his farming as before – and to feed his father and mother and Malanya.

2

Now the Old Devil was most annoyed that the three brothers had not quarrelled over the divvying up, but had parted affectionately. So he summoned the three imps. "Now listen to me," he said. "There are three brothers:

Semyon the Soldier, Taras the Big-Belly and Ivan the Fool. They all should have quarrelled, but instead they're living in peace and on good terms. The fool upset all of my plans. I want the three of you to go out and take on the three of them. Get them so worked up they'll tear each other's eyes out. Can you do that?"

"We can do it," the three imps said.

"How will you go about it?"

"Like this," they said. "First we'll make them so poor they won't have a crust of bread to nibble on. Then we'll throw them together in a heap, and they'll start fighting."

"All right," the Old Devil said. "I see you know your business. Get going. And don't come back until all three of them are at loggerheads. Otherwise I'll skin all three of you alive."

The imps went off to a swamp to discuss how they should go at this business. They argued and argued, each one trying to get the easiest job. Finally they decided to draw straws to determine who would take on whom. And if one finished his job first, he was supposed to help the others. They drew straws, and then set a time when they would again meet in the swamp to find out who had finished his job, and whom he should help.

When the time came, the imps assembled in the swamp as agreed. Each one began to explain how things were going with him. The first imp started telling about Semyon the Soldier.

"My job is coming along fine," he said. "Tomorrow Semyon will be going home to his father."

His brothers began to question him. "How did you manage it?" they asked.

"Well," he said, "the first thing I did was to instil so much bravery into Semyon that he promised his Tsar he would conquer the whole world. So the Tsar made him a commanding general and sent him to do battle with the King of India. The battle lines were drawn up. But during the night I dampened all the gunpowder that Semyon's army had. Then I went to the King of India, and for him I made more straw soldiers than can possibly be imagined. When Semyon's soldiers saw the straw soldiers coming at them from every side, they took fright. Semyon gave orders to fire, but the artillery and the rifles wouldn't discharge. Semyon's soldiers panicked and fled like sheep, and the King of India defeated them.

"Now Semyon the Soldier is in disgrace; the people have taken away his estate, and they intend to execute him tomorrow. I have only one day's work left – to get him out of prison so he can run home. My job will be finished then. Now tell me, which one of you two needs help?"

The second imp – the one assigned to Taras – began telling about his work. "I don't need any help," he said. "My job has come along very well too. Taras won't hold out for more than another week. The first thing I did was to make his belly still bigger and fill him with envious greed. He developed so much envy for the things other people had that he wanted to buy whatever he saw. He spent all his money buying immense quantities of things, and he's still buying – except that now it's with borrowed money. He is already in so much debt that he won't be able to worm his way out of it. A week from now his payments will be due, but I'll turn all his merchandise into manure. He won't be able to pay, and he'll go home to his father."

Then they began to question the third imp about Ivan. "How is your work coming along?" they asked.

"To tell the truth," he said, "it isn't going very well. The first thing I did was to spit in his jug of kvass so he'd have a stomach ache. Then I went to the field he was ploughing, and pounded the earth until it was as hard as stone, so he wouldn't be able to plough it. I was sure he couldn't. But, fool that he is, he came with his wooden plough and began making a furrow. He groaned with the pain in his stomach, but he kept right on ploughing. I broke that one plough, but the idiot went home, rigged up another one, and started ploughing again. I crawled under the ground and grabbed onto the ploughshare, but there was no holding it back: the fool leant hard on the plough, and the ploughshare was sharp – it cut my hands all over. By now he's ploughed almost the whole field; there's only one little strip left. Come and help me, fellows," he said, "because if we don't get the better of him, all our labour will be lost. If that fool keeps on farming, none of them will be really up against it, because he'll feed both of his brothers."

3

Ivan had ploughed almost all of the fallow land. Only one little strip was left, and he went out to finish it. His stomach ached, but the ploughing had to be done.

Ivan let the harness ropes go slack, flipped the plough over, and started ploughing. He had just made one furrow and headed back when the plough began to drag as if it was caught on a root. Actually, it was the imp, who had twined his legs around the ploughshare and was holding it back. That's funny, Ivan thought. There wasn't any root there before, but now there is.

He reached down into the furrow and felt something soft. He grabbed it, and pulled it out. It was black, like a root; but on that root something was wriggling. Lo and behold! A live imp!

"Just look at you!" said Ivan. "How disgusting!"

He raised his hand, and was about to smash the imp on the plough handle, but the imp squealed: "Don't hit me! I'll do whatever you want!"

"What will you do for me?"

"Anything you want – just tell me."

Ivan scratched himself. "My belly aches," he said. "Can you fix it?"

"Yes," said the imp.

"Well then, fix it."

The imp bent over and scratched around in the furrow with his claws. He scratched around some more, then he pulled out a little three-pronged root and handed it to Ivan. "Here," he said. "Whenever anybody eats one of these little roots, all his pains go away."

Ivan took it, tore it apart, and swallowed one of the rootlets. His stomach ache vanished immediately.

The imp began to plead again. "Let me go," he said. "If you do, I'll jump into the earth and never walk on top of it again."

"Well, why not?" said Ivan. "I don't care what you do, God knows."

No sooner had Ivan mentioned God than the imp sank down into the earth like a stone into water, and nothing remained but a hole. Ivan stuck the other two roots in his cap and set about finishing his ploughing. When he had ploughed the rest of the strip, he flipped the plough over and went home.

He unharnessed the mare, and went into the hut. There sat his older brother, Semyon the Soldier, and his wife – eating supper. Semyon's estate had been taken away from him; he had barely managed to escape from prison and he had come running home to live with his father.

When Semyon saw Ivan he said, "I've come to live with you. Feed me and my wife until a new position opens up for me."

"Well, why not?" said Ivan. "You're welcome to live here."

He was about to sit down on the bench, but the high-born lady objected to his smell. "I simply cannot eat," she said, "at the same table as a stinking peasant."

And Semyon the Soldier said, "My lady says you don't smell good. You'd better eat in the hallway."

"Well, why not?" said Ivan. "Anyway, it's time for the night watch. I have to put the mare out to pasture."

He took some bread, picked up his coat, and went out for the night watch in the pasture.

4

Semyon the Soldier's imp, having finished his job that night, came looking for Ivan's imp to help him get the better of the fool. He came to the ploughed field and looked and looked for his brother, but found only a hole in the ground. Well, he thought, it looks as though my brother ran into trouble, so I'll have to take his place. And the ploughing is all done, so I'll have to get the better of the fool while he's mowing the hay.

The imp went to the meadow and flooded the entire crop of hay so that it was all covered with mud. At daybreak, Ivan returned from his night watch, sharpened a scythe, and went to the meadow to mow. He had only swung the scythe a couple of times when it became dull and in need of sharpening again. Ivan struggled and struggled, but finally he said, "Enough of this. I'll go home and get the whetstone and bring it out here with me. And I'll bring along a loaf of bread. Even if it takes me a week of hard work, I'm not leaving until this hay is mowed."

The imp heard him, and thought, "This fool is a tough nut to crack. I'll have to try some other tricks."

Ivan came back, whetted the scythe, and began to mow. The imp crawled into the uncut hay and began grabbing the scythe by the heel, driving the tip of the blade into the ground. It was hard going for Ivan, but he mowed all of the hay except one small patch in a bog. The imp crawled into the bog, thinking to himself, "Even if I get my paws cut off, I won't let him finish mowing."

Ivan went into the swamp. He could see that the grass there wasn't thick; and yet he couldn't cut through it. He grew angry and started swinging with all his might. The imp began to give up – he just couldn't get out of the way fast enough. Seeing it was no use, he hid himself in a bush. Ivan swung the scythe and grazed the bush, cutting off half the imp's tail.

When he had finished mowing the hay, Ivan told his sister to rake it while he went to mow the rye.

He went to the rye field with his sickle; but the bobtailed imp had got there first and tangled up the rye so badly that the sickle wouldn't cut. Ivan went back, brought a reaping hook, and started cutting down the rye with that. He reaped all of it.

"Now," he said, "it's time to go to work on the oats."

The bobtailed imp heard him and thought, "I didn't get the better of him on the rye, but I will on the oats. Just wait till morning!"

The next morning the imp hurried out to the oat field, but the oats were already cut. Ivan had harvested them at night. The imp was furious. He said to himself, "That fool has cut me up and worn me out. Not even in war did I ever see such calamities. He never sleeps, damn him! You just can't keep up with him. But now I'll get into the shocks and rot all of them for him."

So the imp went up to a shock of rye, crawled in among the sheaves, and began rotting them. He warmed them up, but he warmed himself at the same time and dozed off.

Meanwhile, Ivan harnessed the mare and went with his sister to bring in the rye. He came to that particular shock where the imp was sleeping and began pitching the sheaves onto the cart. He pitched up two of them, stuck his fork in again – and jabbed the imp right in the rear end! He raised up the fork, and – lo and behold! – on the prongs was a live imp, and a bobtailed one at that, wriggling, making horrible faces, and trying to get off the hook!

"Just look at you!" Ivan said. "How disgusting! Are you back again?"

"I'm not the same one," the imp said. "That was my brother. And I used to be with your own brother Semyon."

"Well," said Ivan, "whoever you are, you're going to get the same thing he got." And he was about to smash him on the edge of the hay rack when the imp began to plead with him.

"Let me go!" he said. "I won't bother you any more, and I'll do whatever you want me to."

"And what can you do?"

"Well," he said, "for one thing I can make soldiers out of almost anything."

"But what are they good for?"

"Why, for whatever you want. They can do anything."

"Can they play tunes?"

"Oh, yes!"

"Well then, make some."

Then the imp said, "Take that sheaf of rye there and shake it over the ground, bottom down, and then say: *By my bondman's decree, let this sheaf cease to be. And let there be as many soldiers as there are straws in thee.*"

Ivan took the sheaf and shook it over the ground, uttering the words the imp had told him to say. The sheaf burst apart and turned into soldiers, with a drummer and buglers marching in front.

Ivan laughed. "Just look at that!" he said. "How clever! Just dandy! The girls will enjoy it."

"Well, then," the imp said, "let me go now."

"No," said Ivan, "I'll make them out of straw. That way, the grain won't be wasted. Show me how to turn them back into a sheaf. Then I'll thresh it."

So the imp told him: "Just say: *Let there be as many straws as there are soldiers now. By my bondman's decree, let this sheaf once more be.*"

Ivan said the words, and the sheaf reappeared.

"Now let me go," the imp said.

"Well, why not?"

Ivan hooked him onto the edge of the hay rack, took hold of him with one hand, and pulled him off the pitchfork. "God be with you," he said.

As soon as he mentioned God, the imp sank into the ground like a stone into water, and nothing remained but a hole.

Ivan went home, and there he found his other brother, Taras, sitting at supper with his wife. Taras the Big-Belly hadn't managed to pay his debts, and had run home to his father. When he saw Ivan he said, "What do you say, Ivan? Can you feed me and my wife until I get back on my feet?"

"Well, why not?" said Ivan. "You're welcome to live here."

He took off his coat and sat down at the table. But the merchant's daughter said: "I can't eat at the same table as the fool. He reeks," said she, "of sweat."

And Taras the Big-Belly said, "Ivan, you smell bad. You'd better go eat in the hallway."

"Well, why not?" said Ivan. He took some bread and headed out of the door. "Besides," he said, "it's time to pasture the mare for the night."

5

That night Taras's imp came to help his brothers get the better of Ivan the Fool. He came to the ploughed field and looked and looked for them, but there wasn't anyone there – just a hole in the ground. He went to the hayfield, and in the bog he found a tail, and near a shock of rye he found another hole. "Well," he told himself, "it's plain to see that they ran into trouble. I'll have to take their place and get to work on the fool."

The imp went looking for Ivan. But Ivan had already finished the work in the harvest fields and was in the grove cutting down trees. (Ivan's two brothers had begun to feel cramped living together, so they had told the fool to keep the hut for himself and go out and fell some trees and build new houses for them.)

The imp hurried to the grove, crawled up into the branches of a tree, and began to hinder Ivan at his work. Ivan had undercut a tree so it would fall clear, and then chopped through it. But it fell the wrong way and got caught in some branches. He cut off a pole, pried the tree loose, and finally managed to bring it down. He started felling another tree, and the same thing happened: he struggled and struggled, and barely managed to free it. He went to work on a third tree, and again the same thing happened.

Ivan had intended to cut down about fifty young trees; but night settled over the farm before he had even brought down a dozen. And he was exhausted. Steam rose from him and spread through the woods like a fog, but still he would not quit. He undercut one more tree, but then his back began to ache so painfully that he couldn't stand it. He drove his axe into the tree and sat down to rest.

When the imp saw that Ivan had stopped working, he was delighted. Well, he thought, he's worn out – he'll give up now, and I can get a rest too.

He sat down astride a branch, rejoicing. But Ivan got up, pulled out his axe, hauled it up and hit the tree from the other side with such force that it immediately began to sway, and then crashed down. The imp was caught off guard; he couldn't get his leg free in time. The branch broke off, and trapped the imp by his paw.

Ivan had begun stripping the tree when, lo and behold! a live imp!

Ivan was amazed. "Just look at you!" he said. "How disgusting! Are you back again?"

"I'm not the same one," he said. "I was with your brother Taras."

"Well, whoever you are, you're going to get the same thing he got!"

Ivan brandished his axe, and was about to beat the imp with the butt end.

"Don't hit me!" he pleaded. "I'll do whatever you want."

"And what can you do?"

"Well," he said, "for one thing I can create money for you – as much as you want."

"Well, then," said Ivan, "make some."

So the imp showed him how. "Take a leaf from this oak tree," he said, "and rub it in your hands; gold will fall to the ground."

Ivan took some leaves and rubbed them; a shower of gold fell on the ground. "This is dandy," he said, "for playing games with children."

"Then let me go," the imp said.

"Well, why not?" He took his pole and pried the imp free, saying, "I don't care what you do, God knows."

No sooner had he mentioned God than the imp sank into the ground like a stone into water, and nothing remained but a hole.

6

The brothers had built their houses and were living separately. Meanwhile, having finished with the harvest work and brewed some beer, Ivan invited his brothers to celebrate with him. But they wouldn't come. "We are not accustomed," they said, "to joining in the celebrations of peasants."

So Ivan invited some peasants and their wives. He himself drank heartily, grew tipsy, and went out into the street where people were singing and dancing. He went up to them and told the women to sing a song in his praise. "Then," he said, "I'll give you something you've never seen before in your life." The women laughed, and sang a song praising him. When they had finished they said, "Well, let's have it!"

"I'll bring it," he said, "right now." And he grabbed a seed bag and ran off to the woods.

"He really is a fool!" the women said, laughing. And they forgot about him. But behold! Ivan was running back, carrying the seed bag full of something.

"Should I give it out?"

"Yes, give it out!"

Ivan took a handful of gold and threw it at the women. Lord, how they rushed to pick it up! And up came the men, scrambling and fighting over it. One old woman was almost crushed to death.

Ivan laughed. "Oh, you fools!" he said. "Why crush the old granny? Take it easy – I'll give you more." And he began to scatter more of it. They scrambled for the gold and Ivan emptied the whole bag.

Then he said, "That's all. I'll give you more some other time. Now let's have some songs and dancing."

The women struck up a song.

"Your songs are no good," he said.

"What songs are better?" they asked.

"I'll show you," he said. "Right now."

He went to the barn and got a sheaf of grain. He beat out the grain, stood the sheaf on its bottom end, and tapped it. "Now," he said, "*My serf would as lief thou wert no more a sheaf, but every straw a soldier.*"

The sheaf burst apart, and turned into soldiers playing drums and bugles. Ivan ordered the soldiers to play a march, and then he led them out into the street. The people were amazed. The soldiers played some more tunes, and then Ivan led them back to the barn, saying nobody should follow them. There he turned the soldiers back into a sheaf, and threw it back on the pile. Then he went home and lay down to sleep in the stable.

7

The next morning the eldest brother, Semyon the Soldier, heard about these things and went to see Ivan. "Tell me," he said, "where did you get those soldiers? And where did you take them?"

"Why do you want to know?" Ivan asked.

"What do you mean, *why*? With soldiers, a man can do anything. He can win a kingdom for himself."

Ivan was astonished. "Is that so? Why didn't you tell me a long time ago? I'll make you as many soldiers as you want. Thank goodness we threshed a lot – I mean the girl and me."

Ivan took his brother to the barn and said, "Look, I'll make them for you, but then you'll have to take them away from here. Because if we had to feed them they'd gobble up the whole village in one day."

Semyon the Soldier promised to lead the troops away, and Ivan began to make them. He tapped one sheaf on the floor – and there was a company. He tapped another sheaf – and there was another company. He made so many that they covered an entire field.

"Well, that should be about enough, shouldn't it?"

Semyon was overjoyed. He said, "Yes, that's enough. Thank you, Ivan."

"All right. If you need any more, just come back here and I'll make more. I have a lot of straw right now."

Semyon the Soldier immediately gave orders to his troops, mustered them in proper fashion, and went off to make war.

No sooner had Semyon the Soldier left than Taras the Big-Belly showed up. He, too, had heard about what happened the day before, and he asked his brother: "Tell me, where did you get those gold coins? If I had that much cash on hand, I'd use it to bring in money from all over the world!"

Ivan was astonished. "Is that so? You should have told me a long time ago. I'll rub you as much money as you want."

His brother was delighted. "Give me about three sacks of it."

"Well, why not?" said Ivan. "Let's go to the woods. But you'd better harness up the horse first. You won't be able to carry it by yourself."

They went into the woods, and Ivan began to rub leaves from the oak tree. Soon there was a big pile of gold.

"That should be about enough, shouldn't it?"

Taras was overjoyed. "It will do for the time being," he said. "Thank you, Ivan."

"All right," said Ivan. "If you need any more, just come back here and I'll rub some more – there are plenty of leaves left."

Taras the Big-Belly gathered up the money – a whole cartload – and went off to trade.

So the two brothers went away: Semyon to wage war, and Taras to trade. Semyon the Soldier won a kingdom for himself, and Taras the Big-Belly made a heap of money buying and selling.

The two brothers got together and revealed their secrets to each other: where Semyon had got his soldiers, and where Taras had got his money.

And Semyon the Soldier said to his brother, "I have conquered a kingdom for myself, and I live well, but I don't have enough money to feed my soldiers."

Taras the Big-Belly said, "And I have made a great heap of money. But there's just one trouble: I don't have anybody to guard it."

Then Semyon the Soldier said, "Let's go and see brother Ivan. I'll order him to make more soldiers, and then I'll give them to you to guard your money. And you can order him to rub me more money so I'll have the wherewithal to feed my soldiers."

And so they went to see Ivan. When they got there, Semyon said: "Brother mine, I still don't have enough soldiers. Make me some more – from as many sheaves as there are in a couple of shocks, say."

Ivan shook his head. "You're wasting your breath," he said. "I won't make any more soldiers for you."

"But why? After all, you promised."

"I know. But I won't make any more."

"But why won't you, you fool?"

"Because your soldiers killed a man dead. The other day when I was going near the road I saw a woman coming down the road hauling a coffin, and she was wailing. 'Who died?' I asked her. And she said, 'Semyon's soldiers killed my husband in the war.' I thought the soldiers would play tunes, but they've killed a man dead. So I won't give you any more."

And he stood firm, and made no more soldiers.

Then Taras the Big-Belly began pleading with Ivan the Fool to make him more gold coins.

Ivan shook his head. "You're wasting your breath," he said. "I won't make any more."

"But why won't you, you fool?"

"Because your gold pieces took away Mikhailovna's cow."

"What do you mean, *took it away*?"

"They just took it away, that's all. Mikhailovna had a cow, and her children used to drink the milk. The other day they came to me asking for milk. I asked them, 'Where is your cow?' And they said, 'Taras the Big-Belly's steward came and gave Mamma three pieces of gold, and she gave him the cow, so now we don't have any milk to drink.' I thought you only wanted to play games with the gold pieces, but you took away the children's cow. So I won't give you any more."

And the fool stood firm, and wouldn't give any more.

So the two brothers went away, and began to consider how they might help each other in their troubles. And Semyon said, "I'll tell you what we'll do. You give me money to feed my soldiers, and I'll give you half of my kingdom and soldiers to guard your money."

Taras agreed. The brothers divided their possessions, and both became tsars, and both were rich.

8

Meanwhile, Ivan lived at home, feeding his father and mother and working in the fields with the mute girl.

Now it happened that Ivan's old watchdog got sick, became mangy, and was about to die. Ivan felt sorry for her. He got some bread from his sister, Malanya, put it in his cap, took it out to the dog, and threw it to her. But the cap was torn, and along with the bread, a root fell out. The aged dog gobbled it up together with the bread. No sooner had it swallowed the root, than it jumped up and started to play — wagging its tail and barking. It had recovered completely!

Ivan's father and mother saw this, and they were amazed. "How did you cure the dog?" they asked.

And Ivan said, "I had two little roots that cure any pain, and it gobbled up one of them."

At that same time it happened that the Tsar's daughter fell ill. The Tsar caused it to be announced in all cities and hamlets that whosoever cured her would receive an award and, if he were a bachelor, would be given her hand in marriage. The announcement was made in Ivan's village too.

His father called Ivan in and said to him, "Did you hear what the Tsar has announced? You were saying that you had one of those little roots left. Go and cure the Tsar's daughter, and you'll be happy the rest of your life."

"Well, why not?" he said.

And Ivan got ready to go. His father and mother helped him dress up, and he had just stepped out of

153

the door when he saw a beggar woman with a crippled arm. "They tell me," she said, "that you can cure people. Heal my arm – otherwise I can't even put on my boots myself."

And Ivan said, "Well, why not?"

He took the little root, gave it to the beggar woman, and told her to swallow it. She swallowed it, was cured, and began waving her arm.

Ivan's father and mother came out to accompany him on his trip to see the Tsar. When they heard he had given his last root away and had nothing left to cure the Tsar's daughter with, they began to upbraid him. "You took pity on the beggar woman," they said, "but for the Tsar's daughter you have no pity!"

Ivan began to feel sorry for the Tsar's daughter too. He harnessed up the horse, threw some straw into the cart and climbed in, ready to set off.

"Where are you going, fool?"

"To heal the Tsar's daughter."

"When you have nothing to heal her with?"

"Well, why not?" he said, and gave the horse a flick of the reins.

He arrived at the Tsar's palace, and no sooner had he set foot on the steps than the Tsar's daughter recovered. The Tsar was overjoyed. He summoned Ivan, had him dressed in fine clothing, and rewarded him. "Be my son-in-law," he said.

"Well, why not?" said Ivan.

So he married the Tsar's daughter. Not long afterwards the Tsar died, and Ivan became Tsar. So now all three brothers were tsars.

9

The three brothers lived and reigned.

The eldest brother, Semyon the Soldier, lived very well. He drafted real soldiers to add to his straw soldiers. He decreed that throughout his realm one household out of every ten must supply a soldier; and that every soldier must be tall, physically fit and clear-eyed. He recruited many such soldiers, and trained them all. Whenever anybody opposed his designs, he immediately dispatched these soldiers, and did whatever he wanted. So everybody began to fear him.

His life was most pleasant. Whatever he thought of, or whatever he laid eyes on, was his. He would send out his soldiers, and they would seize and bring back whatever he wanted.

Taras the Big-Belly also lived very well. He had not wasted the money he had got from Ivan, but had made lots more with it. In his kingdom he had set up a fine system. He kept his money in coffers, and collected a poll tax, and a vodka tax, and a beer tax, and a wedding tax, and a funeral tax, and a tax for travelling on foot, and a tax for travelling on horseback, and a tax on bast shoes, and a tax on leg wrappings, and a tax on dress trimmings. And whatever he took a mind to was his. For money, people would procure anything for him and do anything for him, because everybody needs money.

Ivan the Fool didn't live badly either. As soon as he had buried his father-in-law he took off all his royal attire, gave it to his wife to put away in a trunk, and got back into his peasant's shirt, trousers and bast shoes, and got ready to work. "I'm bored," he said.

"I'm getting a paunch, don't have any appetite, and I can't sleep."

He sent for his mother and father and sister, the mute girl, and started working again.

"But you're the Tsar!" people told him.

"Well, what's the difference?" he said. "Tsars have to eat too."

A cabinet minister came to him and said, "We don't have any money to pay salaries to our officials."

"Well, what's the difference?" he said. "Don't pay them."

"But then they won't perform their official duties."

"Well, what's the difference? Let them stop performing their governmental duties, and they'll be more free to work. Let them haul away the horse manure – they've piled up enough of it."

People came to Ivan to try lawsuits. One of them said: "That man stole my money."

And Ivan said, "Well, why not? That shows he needed it."

Everybody realized that he was a fool. Even his wife told him: "They say you're a fool."

"Well, why not?" he said.

His wife pondered and pondered, but she was a fool too. "Why should I go against my husband?" she said. "Where the needle goes, the thread must follow."

So she took off her royal robes, put them away in a trunk, and went to the mute girl to learn how to work. She learnt, and began helping her husband.

And all the clever people left Ivan's realm. Only the fools remained. Nobody had any money. They lived, worked, fed themselves, and fed all the good people.

10

Now the Old Devil waited and waited to hear from the imps how they had undone the three brothers, but there was no news. So he went to find out for himself. He looked and looked, but didn't find anything anywhere, except three holes. "Well," he thought, "it is plain to see that they did not succeed."

He started investigating, but the three brothers were no longer in their old places. He found them in their various kingdoms, all living and reigning. The Old Devil was highly incensed. "Very well then," he thought, "I'll take care of this matter myself!"

First he went to see Tsar Semyon. But the Old Devil did not keep his own form: he changed himself into an army commander first.

"I've heard, Tsar Semyon," he said, "that you are a great soldier. I myself am well skilled in such matters, and would like to serve you."

Tsar Semyon began to question him, and saw that he was a clever man; so he took him into his service.

The new commander began to teach Semyon how to build up a strong army. "In the first place," he said, "you'll have to draft more soldiers – otherwise you'll have a lot of no-good idlers in your realm. You must draft all of the young men without exception. Then you'll have an army five times bigger than it is now. In the second place, you must get new small arms and artillery. I will provide you with small arms that will fire a hundred bullets at once, so that they scatter like peas. And I will provide you with artillery pieces whose fire will simply incinerate things. Men, horses, walls or whatever – all will go up in flames."

Tsar Semyon paid heed to his new army commander. He gave orders that all young men without exception should be drafted into the army; and he had new munitions plants built. He had new firearms and cannons manufactured, and immediately went to war with the king of a neighbouring country. As soon as the other troops came forth to meet his, Tsar Semyon commanded his soldiers to fire their bullets and unleash their artillery on them. In an instant, half of the troops were crippled or incinerated. The neighbouring king took fright, surrendered, and handed over his realm. Tsar Semyon was delighted.

"Now," said he, "I will conquer the King of India."

But the King of India had heard about Tsar Semyon and adopted all his new ideas, adding a few of his own. In addition to the young men, he drafted unmarried women besides, and his army grew even larger than Tsar Semyon's. In addition to copying all of Tsar Semyon's small arms and artillery, he had thought up the idea of flying through the air and hurling bombs from above.

Tsar Semyon set out to wage war on the King of India, thinking he would do battle in the same way as before. But what works once doesn't always work twice. The King of India, even before Semyon's troops could come within firing range, sent his women soldiers through the air to hurl down bombs from above. The women sprayed bombs on Semyon's army like borax on cockroaches. The whole army took flight, and Semyon was left alone. The King of India took over Semyon's empire, and Semyon the Soldier escaped as best he could.

Having finished off this particular brother, the Old Devil went on to Tsar Taras. He turned himself into a

158

merchant, and settled in Taras's realm. There he set up a business, and began spending money freely, paying the highest prices for everything. Everybody in the country rushed to get some of his money. They got so much money that they settled their debts and even began paying their taxes on time.

Tsar Taras was delighted. "Thanks to this merchant," he told himself, "I'll have even more money than before, and my life will be better than ever."

And Tsar Taras began to dream up new schemes. He decided to build himself a new palace. He notified the people that they should bring him lumber and stone and come to work on the project, and he offered high prices for everything, thinking they would come in flocks to work for his money, as before. But what do you think? They all took their lumber and stone to the merchant, and the workmen all flocked to him. Tsar Taras offered higher rates, but the merchant went still higher. Tsar Taras had a lot of money, but the merchant had even more; and he outbid the royal offer. The Tsar's palace was started, but never completed.

Tsar Taras had planned a park for himself. When autumn came, he sent for people to come and plant the trees and shrubs. But nobody came: everybody was busy digging a pond for the merchant.

Winter came. Tsar Taras decided to buy some sables for a new fur coat. He sent a man to buy them; but the man came back and said, "There aren't any sables. The merchant has all the furs. He paid a higher price and made rugs out of the sables."

Tsar Taras needed to buy some stallions. He sent some men out to buy them, but they came back and said the

159

merchant now had all the good stallions: he was using them to carry water for his pond.

So all of the Tsar's enterprises came to a standstill. All of the people were working for the merchant, not the Tsar. Their only dealings with him was when they paid him their taxes – in money they had got from the merchant.

Tsar Taras had amassed so much money he didn't know where to put it, yet life was becoming miserable for him. He had long ago stopped dreaming up schemes and just wanted to survive somehow; but he couldn't manage even that. There was a shortage of everything. His cooks and coachmen and other servants all left him and went to the merchant. He even began to run out of food. When he sent to the market for something or other, there never was any: the merchant had bought up everything. Only one thing kept coming the Tsar's way: money from taxes.

Tsar Taras waxed furious: he banished the merchant from his realm. But the merchant settled directly across the border. Just as before, the merchant's money attracted everything to him and away from the Tsar.

The Tsar was in a really bad way. He hadn't eaten for days, and rumour had it that the merchant was boasting he was going to buy the Tsar's wife. Tsar Taras got panicky and didn't know which way to turn.

Semyon the Soldier came to him and said, "I need your help. The King of India defeated me."

But Tsar Taras, too, was at the end of his rope. "I haven't eaten for two days myself," he said.

160

11

Having polished off both brothers, the Old Devil turned to Ivan. He changed himself into an army commander, went to see Ivan, and began trying to persuade him to raise an army. "It is not fitting," said he, "that a tsar should have no army. You have only to order me, and I will gather soldiers from among your people and form an army."

Ivan heard him out. "Well, why not?" he said. "Go ahead. But teach them to play their tunes a little better. That's what I like."

The Old Devil went through Ivan's realm trying to recruit volunteers. He announced that all who came to get their heads shaved and join the army would be given a bottle of vodka and a red cap.

Ivan's fools just laughed. "We have all the liquor we want," they said. "We make it ourselves. And our women make us all the different kinds of caps we want. They even make caps of many colours, with tassels to boot."

So nobody would enlist. The Old Devil came to Ivan and said: "Your fools won't volunteer. We'll have to bring them in by force."

"Well, why not?" Ivan said. "Go ahead and use force."

So the Old Devil announced that all of the fools had to come and enlist as soldiers, and that whoever did not would be put to death by Ivan.

The fools came to the commander and said: "You tell us that if we don't enlist as soldiers our tsar will put us to death. But you don't tell us what will happen to us in the army. They say soldiers get killed to death."

"Yes, that does happen."

161

When the fools heard this, they grew stubborn. "We won't enlist," they said. "It's better to be killed at home if it's going to happen one way or the other."

"You're fools!" said the Old Devil. "Such fools! A soldier may or may not get killed. But if you don't enlist, Tsar Ivan will be sure to have you killed."

The fools thought it over and went to see Tsar Ivan the Fool and ask him about it. "An army commander came," they said, "and ordered all of us to join the army. 'If you go into the army,' he told us, 'you may not get killed. But if you don't join, Tsar Ivan will be sure to have you killed.' Is that true?"

Ivan laughed. "How could I, all by myself, put all of you to death? If I weren't a fool, I could explain it to you. But I don't understand it myself."

"All right, then," they said. "We won't go."

"Well," said Ivan, "what's the difference? Don't go."

So the fools went to the army commander and said they wouldn't enlist.

The Old Devil saw that his plan wasn't working. He went to the King of Cockroachia and talked himself into his favour. "Let's go to war," he said, "and conquer Tsar Ivan. He doesn't have any money, but he has lots of grain and livestock and other things."

The King of Cockroachia went to war. He raised a big army, put the rifles and cannon into good working order, and marched to the border of Ivan's country.

People came to Ivan and said, "The King of Cockroachia is coming to make war on us."

"Well," said Ivan, "what's the difference? Let him come."

The Cockroachian King crossed the border with his army and sent scouts ahead to reconnoitre.

They looked and looked, but they couldn't find any army. They waited and waited, thinking surely it would show up somewhere. But there was no sign of an army – there was nobody they could fight.

The King of Cockroachia sent troops to capture the villages. They entered one village, and out ran the fools, men and women alike, gaping at the soldiers in astonishment. The soldiers began taking away the fools' grain and cattle. The fools just handed everything over, and not a one of them put up a fight.

The troops went into the next village, and the same thing happened. They marched on for another day, and another, and everywhere the same thing happened: they handed over everything; not a single one put up a fight; and they even invited the soldiers to stay. "Dear friends," they said, "if life is not good in your country, come and live here with us."

The soldiers marched on and on, but they never encountered an army: just people living and feeding themselves and others, never resisting – just inviting them to stay.

The soldiers became bored. They went to their Cockroachian King and said, "We can't fight here. Take us somewhere else. A war would be fine, but this is like slicing jelly. We can't go on with this campaign."

The King of Cockroachia flew into a rage. He commanded his soldiers to overrun the country, lay waste the villages and houses, burn the grain, and slaughter the livestock. "If you disobey my orders," he said, "all of you will be put to death."

The soldiers were frightened and began to carry out the King's orders. They burnt houses and grain, and

163

slaughtered the livestock. But still the fools did not defend themselves: all they did was weep. The old men wept, the old women wept and the little children wept. "Why do you want to hurt us?" they asked. "Why are you foolishly destroying good things? If you need them, why don't you just take them?"

The soldiers couldn't bear it any longer. They refused to go on, and the army fell apart.

12

The Old Devil also went away, having failed to defeat Ivan with the soldiers.

He turned himself into a fine gentleman and came back to settle in Ivan's country. His plan now was to undo Ivan the same way he had undone Taras the Big-Belly: with money.

"I want to do you a favour," he told Ivan, "to teach you some common sense. I'll build a house here, and set up a business."

"Well, why not?" said Ivan. "Go ahead."

The fine gentleman spent the night there; and the next morning he appeared in the public square. He produced a big bag of gold and a sheet of paper. "All you people," he said, "live like pigs. I want to show you how to live properly. You build me a house according to this plan, and I'll supervise your work and pay you in gold coin."

He showed them the gold. The fools were amazed. They had never used money; instead, they bartered or paid one another by working. They marvelled at the gold. "Those are pretty little things," they said.

And they began to exchange their labour and other things for the gentleman's gold pieces. The Old Devil started spending his gold freely, as he had done in Taras's kingdom; and the people began trading all kinds of things, and doing all kinds of work, for his gold.

The Old Devil was elated. "Things are coming along fine," he thought. "Now I'll fix the fool the way I did Taras. I'll buy him out of the running – innards and all!"

But no sooner had the fools garnered their gold pieces than they gave them away to the women for necklaces. The girls plaited them into their braids, and the children played with them in the streets. They all had plenty of them, and they wouldn't take any more. Meanwhile, the fine gentleman's mansion was not yet half built, and his livestock and grain provisions for the coming year had not yet been taken care of. So he sent word that he wanted people to come and work for him, to haul in grain and bring in livestock; and that for every product or every job done, he would pay lots of gold.

But nobody came to work for him, and nobody brought anything to him. A little boy or girl might occasionally stop by with an egg to trade in for gold, but otherwise nobody came, and he began to run out of food. The fine gentleman got very hungry and went through the village trying to buy something for his supper. He went to a peasant's house and offered gold for a hen, but the housewife wouldn't take it. "I have plenty of it already," she said.

He went to a poor old woman's and offered gold coins for a herring. "I don't need any of them, kind sir," said she. "I have no children I could give them to as toys, and besides I already have three coins I picked up as curiosities."

He went to an old peasant for bread. But the old peasant wouldn't take any money either.

"I don't need it," he said. "But if you're asking in the name of Christ, just wait a minute and I'll tell my old woman to cut you a slice."

The Old Devil spat and fled from the peasant. Let alone actually begging *in the name of Christ*, just hearing the words hurt him worse than a knife stab.

And so he got no bread either. All the people had all the money they needed. Wherever the Old Devil went, nobody would give anything for money. They all said, "Bring something else to trade, or come and do some work, or else take some food in the name of Christ." But the Old Devil had nothing but money, and he didn't want to work, and he couldn't possibly accept charity in the name of Christ.

He became furious. "I will give you money," he told the fools. "What more do you want? With money you can buy anything and hire any workman."

But they wouldn't listen. "No," they said, "we don't need it. We don't have any bills or taxes to pay, so what do we need money for?"

So the Old Devil went to bed without his supper.

Ivan the Fool heard about all this business. Some people came to him and asked: "What shall we do? There's this fine gentleman who appeared among us: he likes good things to eat and drink; he likes to wear fine clothes; but he doesn't like to work, and he won't beg in the name of Christ. All he does is offer gold pieces to everybody. People used to give him everything he needed, but now they have enough gold pieces and won't give him anything more. What should we do with him? He might starve to death."

Ivan listened to their story. "Well, after all," he said, "he has to be fed. Let him go from farm to farm, like a shepherd."

There was no other choice for him: the Old Devil had to start making the rounds of the farms.

Eventually he came to Ivan's house. He arrived at supper time, and Malanya the Mute was preparing supper. Often before, she had been tricked by lazy people. Since they hadn't been working, they could get there for supper before the others, and then they'd eat up all the porridge. So she had learnt to recognize loafers by the palms of their hands. If a man had calluses on his hands, she would seat him at the table; if not, he'd have to wait for the scraps.

The Old Devil sidled up to the table; but the mute girl seized him by the hands and took a look. There were no calluses: his hands were clean and smooth, with long fingernails. She grunted and dragged him away from the table.

But Ivan's wife said to him, "You must excuse us, fine sir. My sister-in-law doesn't let people sit at the table unless they have callused hands. Just wait a little, and when the others have eaten you can have what's left."

The Old Devil was insulted that at the Tsar's house they were making him eat along with the pigs. He said to Ivan, "That's a stupid law you have in your realm – that everybody has to work with his hands. Do you think it's only with their hands that people work? What do you suppose clever people work with?"

"How should we fools know?" Ivan answered. "We're all used to working mostly with our hands and our backs."

"That's because you're fools. But I'll teach you how to work with your heads. Then you'll realize it's more profitable to work with your head than your hands."

Ivan was astonished. "Well," said he, "it's no wonder we're called fools!"

"However," the Old Devil went on, "it's not so easy — working with your head. You refused to let me eat just now, because I didn't have calluses on my hands. But what you don't realize is that it's a hundred times harder to work with your head. Sometimes your head even splits."

Ivan thought about it a minute. "But then why, my dear friend," said he, "do you make it so hard on yourself? There's nothing easy about getting your head split, that's for sure. You'd be better off doing easy work — with your hands and your back."

Said the Old Devil, "Why do I make it hard on myself? Because I feel sorry for you fools. If I didn't make it hard on myself, you'd remain fools all your lives. But now that I've worked with my head, I can teach you how."

Ivan was very impressed. "You teach us," he said. "And then whenever our hands wear out, we can switch to our heads."

So the Old Devil promised to teach them.

Ivan announced throughout his realm that a fine gentleman had arrived who would teach them all how to work with their heads; and that a man could work more profitably with his head than with his hands, so everybody should come and learn how.

Now a high tower had been built in Ivan's realm, with a straight stairway on the outside, leading up to a lookout platform on the top. Ivan took the gentleman up there so that he would be in full view.

The gentleman stood atop the tower and began to speak. The fools gathered around and gaped. They thought the gentleman would actually demonstrate how to work with your head without using your hands. But all the Old Devil did was talk – explaining how to live without doing any work.

The fools didn't understand a word of it. They watched a bit longer, and then went off to attend to their own business.

The Old Devil stood on top of the tower for one whole day, and then another – talking constantly. He got hungry. But it never occurred to the fools to bring some bread to the tower for him. They figured that if he could work better with his head than with his hands, it would be no trick at all for his head to provide him with bread.

The Old Devil stood up there on the tower for another whole day, still talking. People would come and take a look, then go away. Ivan asked, "Well, how is the gentleman doing? Has he started working with his head yet?"

"Not yet," they told him. "He's still jabbering."

The Old Devil stood on top of the tower for one more day, and began to grow weak. He staggered, and struck his head on a pillar. One of the people saw him topple, and told Ivan's wife. She ran out to the field where her husband was ploughing. "Come and look!" she told him. "They say the gentleman has begun to work with his head."

Ivan marvelled. "Oh?" said he.

He turned his horse around and went to the tower. By the time he got there the Old Devil was already very weak from hunger and was staggering around, knocking his head against the pillars. Just as Ivan got there he stumbled and fell, crashing down the stairway head over heels, counting out each step with his head.

"Well," said Ivan, "the fine gentleman was telling the truth when he said that sometimes his head splits. In his kind of work it isn't calluses you get – it's lumps on the head."

The Old Devil came tumbling down the stairway and rammed his head into the ground at the bottom. Ivan had started towards him to see how much work he had done, when suddenly the earth opened up and the Old Devil fell into it. Only a hole remained.

Ivan scratched himself. "Just look at that! How disgusting! Him again! But he must be the father of all the others – he's a big one."

Ivan still lives to this day, and everybody flocks to his realm to live. His brothers have come there too, and he feeds them.

Whenever anybody comes and says, "Feed us," he says, "Well, why not? Make yourself at home – we have plenty of everything."

But there is this one custom in his realm: if you have calluses on your hands, you're welcome at the table; if you don't, you eat the scraps.

1886

Notes

p. 19, *bublik*: A kind of bagel.

p. 20, *mayor*: A loose equivalent for *gorodnichy*, the appointed "police governor" of the town.

p. 25, *puppet shows*: In Russian, *vertep* – a puppet show on the theme of the Nativity.

p. 28, *Little Russia*: The Ukraine.

p. 31, *laid hands on them*: I.e., impounded them, so as subsequently to demand payment of a fine for use of the pastureland.

p. 36, *making a fig at him*: An offensive hand gesture.

p. 38, *Lyuby, Gary and Popov*: Publishers of cheap illustrated books for the semi-literate.

p. 45, *zertsalo*: The emblem of office under the Russian Empire. It had the shape of a triangular prism, with each facet displaying (under glass) a decree of Peter the Great, and was surmounted by the two-headed eagle.

p. 72, *Anton Prokofyevich Golopuz*: This is the same Anton Prokofyevich who appeared earlier with the last name of "Pupopuz".

p. 73, *"Fools" and "Millers"*: Card games.

p. 103, *generals*: These are "civilian generals", i.e. civil servants whose grade was the equivalent of a general's rank in the military.

p. 106, *an order*: I.e. an official decoration of the kind worn on a ribbon around the neck.

p. 107, *the Fontanka*: The "left branch" of the Neva River (upon whose delta St Petersburg was built). The residential district along the Fontanka was very fashionable.

p. 107, *the Moscow News*: An arch-conservative paper.

p. 110, *the golden sterlet of Sheksna*: The first line of 'Invitation to a Dinner' by Gavriil Derzhavin, the chief Russian poet of the eighteenth century.

p. 111, *holding in its mouth a piece of membrane*: This little piece of membrane has caused infinite difficulties for editors and translators. Saltykov had originally written *kusok zleni*, meaning a piece of parsley (or other greens), but later changed it to *slen'*, meaning (according to the lexicographer Dahl) "a hard membrane resembling translucent skin, with which a fish covers himself in the winter". "Our correspondent from Tula" must have confused the sturgeon with a lungfish!

p. 114, *after a while – maybe a short one, maybe a long one*: A formula recurrent in Russian folk and fairy tales.

p. 114, *state councillor's uniform*: Literally, "of the fourth grade".

p. 114, *it had run down his beard and never got into his mouth*: A very common signature in Russian folk and fairy tales, indicating that the storyteller has become thirsty in the telling of his tale and wouldn't object to a drink.

p. 115, *something no man could write with a pen or tell in a tale*: Another fairy-tale formula.

p. 117, *The Eagle as Patron of the Arts*: The double-headed eagle was the national emblem of the Russian Empire.

p. 122, *Baba-Yaga*: In Russian fairy tales, Baba-Yaga is the archetypal witch.

p. 123, *decorate his whole breast with live cockroaches*: See note to page 106. One type of decoration awarded by the Imperial Government was worn on a ribbon around the neck, another on a broad band across the chest, and so on.

p. 125, *Vasily Kirilych Tredyakovsky*: After the famous eighteenth-century poet of the same name, one of whose duties as secretary of the Russian Academy of Sciences was to compose odes, paeans, etc., for public ceremonies.

1. James Hanley, *Boy*
2. D.H. Lawrence, *The First Women in Love*
3. Charlotte Brontë, *Jane Eyre*
4. Jane Austen, *Pride and Prejudice*
5. Emily Brontë, *Wuthering Heights*
6. Anton Chekhov, *Sakhalin Island*
7. Giuseppe Gioacchino Belli, *Sonnets*
8. Jack Kerouac, *Beat Generation*
9. Charles Dickens, *Great Expectations*
10. Jane Austen, *Emma*
11. Wilkie Collins, *The Moonstone*
12. D.H. Lawrence, *The Second Lady Chatterley's Lover*
13. Jonathan Swift, *The Benefit of Farting Explained*
14. Anonymous, *Dirty Limericks*
15. Henry Miller, *The World of Sex*
16. Jeremias Gotthelf, *The Black Spider*
17. Oscar Wilde, *The Picture Of Dorian Gray*
18. Erasmus, *Praise of Folly*
19. Henry Miller, *Quiet Days in Clichy*
20. Cecco Angiolieri, *Sonnets*
21. Fyodor Dostoevsky, *Humiliated and Insulted*
22. Jane Austen, *Sense and Sensibility*
23. Theodor Storm, *Immensee*
24. Ugo Foscolo, *Sepulchres*
25. Boileau, *Art of Poetry*
26. Kaiser, *Plays Vol. 1*
27. Emile Zola, *Ladies' Delight*
28. D.H. Lawrence, *Selected Letters*
29. Alexander Pope, *The Art of Sinking in Poetry*
30. E.T.A. Hoffmann, *The King's Bride*
31. Ann Radcliffe, *The Italian*
32. Prosper Mérimée, *A Slight Misunderstanding*
33. Giacomo Leopardi, *Canti*
34. Giovanni Boccaccio, *Decameron*
35. Annette von Droste-Hülshoff, *The Jew's Beech*
36. Stendhal, *Life of Rossini*
37. Eduard Mörike, *Mozart's Journey to Prague*
38. Jane Austen, *Love and Friendship*
39. Leo Tolstoy, *Anna Karenina*
40. Ivan Bunin, *Dark Avenues*
41. Nathaniel Hawthorne, *The Scarlet Letter*
42. Sadeq Hedayat, *Three Drops of Blood*
43. Alexander Trocchi, *Young Adam*
44. Oscar Wilde, *The Decay of Lying*
45. Mikhail Bulgakov, *The Master and Margarita*
46. Sadeq Hedayat, *The Blind Owl*
47. Alain Robbe-Grillet, *Jealousy*
48. Marguerite Duras, *Moderato Cantabile*
49. Raymond Roussel, *Locus Solus*
50. Alain Robbe-Grillet, *In the Labyrinth*
51. Daniel Defoe, *Robinson Crusoe*
52. Robert Louis Stevenson, *Treasure Island*
53. Ivan Bunin, *The Village*
54. Alain Robbe-Grillet, *The Voyeur*
55. Franz Kafka, *Dearest Father*
56. Geoffrey Chaucer, *Canterbury Tales*
57. A. Bierce, *The Monk and the Hangman's Daughter*
58. F. Dostoevsky, *Winter Notes on Summer Impressions*
59. Bram Stoker, *Dracula*
60. Mary Shelley, *Frankenstein*
61. Johann Wolfgang von Goethe, *Elective Affinities*
62. Marguerite Duras, *The Sailor from Gibraltar*
63. Robert Graves, *Lars Porsena*
64. Napoleon Bonaparte, *Aphorisms and Thoughts*
65. J. von Eichendorff, *Memoirs of a Good-for-Nothing*
66. Adelbert von Chamisso, *Peter Schlemihl*
67. Pedro Antonio de Alarcón, *The Three-Cornered Hat*
68. Jane Austen, *Persuasion*
69. Dante Alighieri, *Rime*
70. A. Chekhov, *The Woman in the Case and Other Stories*
71. Mark Twain, *The Diaries of Adam and Eve*
72. Jonathan Swift, *Gulliver's Travels*
73. Joseph Conrad, *Heart of Darkness*
74. Gottfried Keller, *A Village Romeo and Juliet*
75. Raymond Queneau, *Exercises in Style*
76. Georg Büchner, *Lenz*
77. Giovanni Boccaccio, *Life of Dante*
78. Jane Austen, *Mansfield Park*
79. E.T.A. Hoffmann, *The Devil's Elixirs*
80. Claude Simon, *The Flanders Road*
81. Raymond Queneau, *The Flight of Icarus*
82. Niccolò Machiavelli, *The Prince*
83. Mikhail Lermontov, *A Hero of our Time*
84. Henry Miller, *Black Spring*
85. Victor Hugo, *The Last Day of a Condemned Man*
86. D.H. Lawrence, *Paul Morel*
87. Mikhail Bulgakov, *The Life of Monsieur de Molière*
88. Leo Tolstoy, *Three Novellas*
89. Stendhal, *Travels in the South of France*
90. Wilkie Collins, *The Woman in White*
91. Alain Robbe-Grillet, *Erasers*
92. Iginio Ugo Tarchetti, *Fosca*
93. D.H. Lawrence, *The Fox*
94. Borys Conrad, *My Father Joseph Conrad*
95. J. De Mille, *A Strange Manuscript Found in a Copper Cylinder*
96. Emile Zola, *Dead Men Tell No Tales*
97. Alexander Pushkin, *Ruslan and Lyudmila*
98. Lewis Carroll, *Alice's Adventures Under Ground*
99. James Hanley, *The Closed Harbour*
100. T. De Quincey, *On Murder Considered as One of the Fine Arts*
101. Jonathan Swift, *The Wonderful Wonder of Wonders*
102. Petronius, *Satyricon*
103. Louis-Ferdinand Céline, *Death on Credit*
104. Jane Austen, *Northanger Abbey*
105. W.B. Yeats, *Selected Poems*
106. Antonin Artaud, *The Theatre and Its Double*
107. Louis-Ferdinand Céline, *Journey to the End of the Night*
108. Ford Madox Ford, *The Good Soldier*
109. Leo Tolstoy, *Childhood, Boyhood, Youth*
110. Guido Cavalcanti, *Complete Poems*
111. Charles Dickens, *Hard Times*
112. Baudelaire and Gautier, *Hashish, Wine, Opium*
113. Charles Dickens, *Haunted House*
114. Ivan Turgenev, *Fathers and Children*
115. Dante Alighieri, *Inferno*
116. Gustave Flaubert, *Madame Bovary*
117. Alexander Trocchi, *Man at Leisure*
118. Alexander Pushkin, *Boris Godunov and Little Tragedies*
119. Miguel de Cervantes, *Don Quixote*
120. Mark Twain, *Huckleberry Finn*
121. Charles Baudelaire, *Paris Spleen*
122. Fyodor Dostoevsky, *The Idiot*
123. René de Chateaubriand, *Atala and René*
124. Mikhail Bulgakov, *Diaboliad*
125. Goerge Eliot, *Middlemarch*
126. Edmondo De Amicis, *Constantinople*
127. Petrarch, *Secretum*
128. Johann Wolfgang von Goethe, *The Sorrows of Young Werther*
129. Alexander Pushkin, *Eugene Onegin*
130. Fyodor Dostoevsky, *Notes from Underground*
131. Luigi Pirandello, *Plays Vol. 1*
132. Jules Renard, *Histoires Naturelles*
133. Gustave Flaubert, *The Dictionary of Received Ideas*
134. Charles Dickens, *The Life of Our Lord*
135. D.H. Lawrence, *The Lost Girl*
136. Benjamin Constant, *The Red Notebook*
137. Raymond Queneau, *We Always Treat Women too Well*
138. Alexander Trocchi, *Cain's Book*
139. Raymond Roussel, *Impressions of Africa*
140. Llewelyn Powys, *A Struggle for Life*
141. Nikolai Gogol, *How the Two Ivans Quarrelled*
142. F. Scott Fitzgerald, *The Great Gatsby*
143. Jonathan Swift, *Directions to Servants*
144. Dante Alighieri, *Purgatory*
145. Mikhail Bulgakov, *A Young Doctor's Notebook*
146. Sergei Dovlatov, *The Suitcase*
147. Leo Tolstoy, *Hadji Murat*
148. Jonathan Swift, *The Battle of the Books*
149. F. Scott Fitzgerald, *Tender Is the Night*
150. A. Pushkin, *The Queen of Spades and Other Short Fiction*
151. Raymond Queneau, *The Sunday of Life*
152. Herman Melville, *Moby Dick*
153. Mikhail Bulgakov, *The Fatal Eggs*
154. Antonia Pozzi, *Poems*
155. Johann Wolfgang von Goethe, *Wilhelm Meister*
156. Anton Chekhov, *The Story of a Nobody*
157. Fyodor Dostoevsky, *Poor People*
158. Leo Tolstoy, *The Death of Ivan Ilyich*
159. Dante Alighieri, *Vita nuova*
160. Arthur Conan Doyle, *The Tragedy of Korosko*
161. Franz Kafka, *Letters to Friends, Family and Editors*
162. Mark Twain, *The Adventures of Tom Sawyer*
163. Erich Fried, *Love Poems*
164. Antonin Artaud, *Selected Works*
165. Charles Dickens, *Oliver Twist*
166. Sergei Dovlatov, *The Zone*
167. Louis-Ferdinand Céline, *Guignol's Band*
168. Mikhail Bulgakov, *Dog's Heart*
169. Rayner Heppenstall, *Blaze of Noon*
170. Fyodor Dostoevsky, *The Crocodile*
171. Anton Chekhov, *Death of a Civil Servant*

www.oneworldclassics.com